THE HISTORIES OF HAYWARD HALL

Also by Alexandria Blaelock

FICTION
That Love Nonsense

MS BLAELOCK'S BOOKS
Stress Free Dinner Parties
Signature Wardrobe Planning
Holistic Personal Finance
Minimally Viable Housekeeping

SHORT STORIES
Alma's Grace
Balancing the Book
Bygone Boyfriend
Carmelita Basingstoke
Fate in Your Hands
Kiss of Death
Lady of the Looking Glass
Life in the Security Directorate
Long Weekend in the Snow
Love in the Security Directorate
Morning Star, Evening Star, Superstar
Needy Bitch
Payton's Run
Phoenix Child
Secret Singer
Shining Star
Ship in a Bottle
Simone Says Hands in the Air
The Day the Schedule Broke
The Guardian's Vigil
Toy Soldiers

THE HISTORIES OF HAYWARD HALL

ALEXANDRIA BLAELOCK

Bluemere Books
MELBOURNE, AUSTRALIA

For permission requests, please contact enquiries@bluemerebooks.com.

Ordering Information:
Discounts are available on quantity purchases. For details, contact orders@bluemerebooks.com.

The Histories of Hayward Hall/Alexandria Blaelock
hardback ISBN: 978-1-925749-51-9
paperback ISBN: 978-1-925749-52-6
digital ISBN: 978-1-925749-53-3

Book Layout © BookDesignTemplates.com

Contents

INTRODUCTION

Welcome to *The Histories of Hayward Hall*.

I live in Melbourne, now the world's second most liveable city. After seven years in top place.

That seems like a whole other universe.

And may or may not have changed after 111 consecutive days of Covid-related lock down.

Is there even a world's most liveable city anymore?

Anyhow, I've been staying at home a lot lately.

Not making sourdough or redecorating, but watching movies.

And coming across mysteriously empty cups of tea.

Theoretically I'm free to travel wherever I like in Australia, but in practical terms, there aren't that many places to visit.

For example, social distancing requirements mean my favourite Korean restaurant can only serve two people at a time for dinner in the restaurant. For their purposes, it's easier, and more lucrative, to just offer take out.

And similarly, Melbourne's historic houses and other attractions. Like Rippon Lea, the house that inspired these stories. All with regulated mask wearing and quantity restrictions in place.

Meanwhile, back at home, I've been watching a lot of horror movies.

Not sure why, it's not like we aren't currently living in a kind of horror scenario.

Hiding away in our homes, venturing out with masks and hand sanitiser only when necessary, waiting for the big bad bug to get us.

The Walking Dead of a different kind.

Though with mask wearing rules relaxing it's harder to know who follows the science and who follows the conspiracy theorists.

Plus, we now have a black puppy that likes hiding in the shadows and leaping out on us.

And it's not like I like horror that much. I only like it in so far as it doesn't feel real. Like *The Twilight Zone*.

Stories that make you think.

And yet, I've been watching a lot of Haunted House movies.

It's stunning how many horror stories rely on the good old evil something embedded in house trope.

Understandable really - I didn't know how much noise my house made until my old dog died.

Fortunately, she is not an evil spirit infesting the house.

And neither is the puppy, much as it seems that way right now.

But I got to thinking, what if the problem in your house was not an evil spirit.

The movie *The Others* had one take on this, but there was still evil at the heart of it.

What, I wondered, if the "ghost" was someone just like you?

Someone who opened the wrong door at the wrong time and couldn't get back.

What if the thing that knocked over your cup just wanted the ghost of a nice hot cup of tea?

And to get back home.

So.

Just for fun.

I wrote five stories about Morag Clementine, who takes an exceedingly well-paid job at Hayward Hall.

And just to prove that Haunted Houses aren't always scary, I've included science fiction, fantasy, mystery and romance as well as a horror story.

Starting with how Morag gets tangled up in the Hall.

Her love affair with Henry Fox.

Young Amelia Fox who investigates her disappearance.

Zoo, the paranormal investigator.

And Kumahl, who discovers the secret to sending her back.

And so, I present to you, five genre spanning original stories about a Haunted House, that's not really haunted.

Alexandria Blaelock
Melbourne, Australia
February, 2021

THE SPACE TIME PARADOX

It was Morag Clementine's first day at Hayward Hall, and so far, she was impressed.

Mystified, but impressed.

She'd arrived late in the afternoon.

There'd been some kind of mix up at the train station, and she'd wheeled her suitcase from the station along the hot, dry, featureless dusty road to the local village.

Fortunately, she was wearing jeans, a light shirt, and her sensible (and comfortable) lace-up brown brogues.

And fortunately, she'd been able to get a taxi up to the main house.

Silhouetted against the setting sun, Hayward Hall just looked wrong. The tiled roof, the feature brick patterns in the walls, the neat windows and imposing doors all looked perfectly fine when taken individually.

Yet somehow there was something not quite right about the overall impression of the house as a whole.

Some kind of blurry smudginess at the edges of her peripheral vision.

She rubbed her eyes and it went away.

The fountain was dry, the formal gardens overgrown, and creatures rustled in the undergrowth.

Hopefully not mice.

Not because she was afraid, but because they were devious little critters that were almost impossible to eliminate once they'd got a foothold.

The sound of rustling was almost obscured by the lorikeets screeching from the trees as they dipped and whirled from branch to branch, and tree to tree.

She'd turned to thank her driver, only to see the car driving away in a plume of dust. Perhaps a little too fast, or perhaps that was her imagination.

She'd looked once more at the Hall, expecting someone to walk out to welcome her, but the house remained as secure as if it had been shut up for decades.

Morag was a practical person, and as there didn't seem much point hanging around waiting for someone to come out, she opened the unlocked front door and went in.

Because to be honest it had been a long day, and she just wanted a cup of tea.

And funnily enough, given she'd been sitting in a train most of the day, she really wanted a sit down too.

Preferably in a cosy armchair.

Hayward Hall smelled of dust and cobwebs, and as she looked around the luxuriously ornamented foyer, she saw a lot of both. And almost immediately added dusting to her list of things to do.

It was cooler inside than out, and coming as she was from the Summer heat, she was grateful. And when the weather got even warmer, she expected she'd appreciate it even more.

The silent grandfather clock had stopped at fourteen minutes past nine, and she couldn't help but look at her watch to see the time was in fact twenty-seven minutes to eight.

Something else for the list.

"Hello," she called and listened for an answer.

There was no sound, and no movement, so she walked a little further in, knocked on the door labelled "Office," and called out again.

Still nothing.

When she opened the door, the displaced air sent clouds of dust into the air nearly choking her.

Clearly, the room hadn't been used to some time, so she closed the door, and spent a few minutes coughing.

She pulled her mobile phone from her pocket, intending to call the agency, but there were no bars and no reception.

She was starting to get annoyed.

Her contract was for a live-in housekeeper, so she walked through the dusty, cobweb festooned house to the back looking for the stairs down to the kitchen.

Ideally, before the light faded.

She left her suitcase by the stairs and descended.

"Hello?" she called as she entered the kitchen.

The basement was dim in the evening light, but with the aid of her phone's light, she was able to find the light switch.

Thankfully the kitchen was clean.

Spotlessly clean.

A modern, fully equipped catering kitchen with gleaming stainless-steel appliances and benchtops arranged around the walls.

She nodded with satisfaction as she noted juicers, mixers and coffee machine in amongst a jumble of other equipment that would need investigation.

At one end, a stove and cooktop, and at the other, an open door leading to the pantry and another for an office.

With what looked to be an exceedingly comfortable floral chintz armchair.

In the centre of the room, on an empty free-standing food preparation area, sat a conspicuous envelope.

On inspection, it contained three pages of spidery handwritten pages that Morag would need her glasses for.

She located the kettle, rinsed it out, filled it with fresh water and put it on to boil. She pulled a cup and saucer from the stacks next to the sink, rifled through the pantry to find tea and sugar, and looked in the fridge for milk.

Fully prepared now, she put her tea on the desk, adjusted the armchair so it was next to the desk, and pulled up a box to use as a footstool

With a sigh, she relaxed into the armchair, took a sip of tea and skimmed the letter.

- Apologies for not greeting her in person.
- Couldn't stay in the Hall a moment longer.
- Bedroom on the first floor, straight down the corridor, last on the left.
- The Young Master in the main bedroom at the front of the house.

- He's ill, don't bother him, unless he calls.
- Breakfast at 9am, Lunch at noon, afternoon tea at 4pm, dinner at 8pm.

Morag gently tapped the letter against her bottom lip.

By that schedule, the Young Master was due his dinner. Did the dinner requirement trump the do not disturb?

She didn't remember seeing any food plated up for his dinner.

She sighed, drank the last of her tea, and got up to check.

Definitely no dinner.

The only thing for it was to check what the Young Master wanted.

She stumped up the first flight of stairs to the ground floor, then collected her suitcase and stumped up the second flight to the first floor.

Took a detour to leave it in her room.

The bed was at least made, though whether it was with clean linen or not didn't matter as much.

She was so tired from her journey that when the time came, she would crawl in there and no doubt fall straight to sleep.

And she managed to find her way back to stand nervously at the Young Master's bedroom door.

Not quite so certain that interrupting him was the right thing to do, regardless of the circumstances.

The agency had told her she was not to bother him.

Likewise, the letter told her not to bother him.

Surely it would be fine.

Just this once. To introduce herself.

To enquire after his dinner needs.

She took a step back and away from the door, perhaps the last housekeeper had already prepared and delivered him a plate of dinner.

And done all the washing up and putting away afterwards.

It wasn't like she officially started work until the morning.

She was about to take another step back when she heard his voice through the door, "come."

Surprisingly deep and resonant.

With the title of the Young Master, she'd half expected a boy, though logically he must be at least 18 to be living in this big house on his own.

Well, not alone as such, but young boys required a different kind of housekeeper.

Someone who usually went with the title of Nanny.

The voice sounded more in the line of thirtyish if ever a voice could suggest an age.

Morag wiped her suddenly sweaty palms on her jeans and then smoothed down her hair.

It occurred to her that she was alone in a big house full of dust and cobwebs.

Where there was no mobile reception.

Perhaps it was wiser to keep backing away, and then run from the place as fast as she could. Just as the taxi driver and previous housekeeper had.

However.

The pay was insanely good, and the benefits weren't bad either.

She straightened her spine and pulled her shoulders back.

"I'm coming in," she said, just as much for her sake as for his, turned the knob and stepped through the doorway into a dining room.

A dining room comprising of small candlelit tables dressed in white cloths, with cutlery for at least four courses and wine glasses to match.

Which wasn't quite right, because this was supposed the be the Young Master's bedroom.

As she turned to check the door behind her, a couple walked past, looking quizzically at her.

Probably the same as she was looking at them given, they looked to be taking a break from filming something like a *Great Gatsby* adaptation, leaving a Hot Set behind them.

She refused to feel out of place in her jeans.

Morag could see through the open door behind her, to the corridor with its dirty pale blue carpet, yellow flocked wallpaper and an incredibly ugly brown waterscape of ducks flying over a pond.

And in the bedroom...

No.

In the dining room...

Walls of mirrors reflected the light from crystal chandeliers hanging from a painted, highly ornamented ceiling. Edwardian upholstered chairs in red matched the carpet and curtains.

Here and there, at other tables, there were more *Great Gatsby* extras. Eating. Drinking. Laughing.

Smoking.

She could still see the corridor she'd entered from, and when she peered around the frame to see the back of the door, there was no door at all. She was looking at the dining room.

She was about to walk back through the door, and close it behind her, when the surprisingly deep and resonant voice said, "Morag, don't be afraid."

"No, Young Master," she said, not turning away from the door, "why would I be afraid when your first-floor bedroom door leads into a hotel dining room? Clearly, I'm hallucinating, and need my rest more than you do."

"It's all right Morag. You're not hallucinating."

She snorted and turned to look at him.

His perfectly ordinary brown hair and eyes. Hands in the pant pockets of his perfectly ordinary Edwardian styled suit. His perfectly ordinary brown brogues.

His slightly smiling face.

"Is there really a hotel dining room in your bedroom then?"

"Not usually Morag," he shifted his weight from foot to foot, as if preparing to capture her, "though there's not always a bed either."

"Are you trying to hypnotise me, what with using my name all the time?"

He snorted, "not at all. I'm trying to sound soothing and reassuring so you won't run screaming out of the house."

"So, I'll ask you again, is there really a hotel inside your room?"

"Not as such," he pulled out a chair from the nearest table, "why don't you sit down and we can talk about it?"

She put her hands on her hips, "now you sound like you're trying to con me."

"What can I say to reassure you?"

"Can I leave the door open?"

"There's no need, but if it makes you feel more comfortable, then feel free."

She glanced back into the corridor.

There was no doubt wherever she was looked more attractive than the house. And wherever she was, looked like there was food and alcohol she didn't have to prepare herself.

Or do the dishes.

She shrugged and took the few steps to the table. He held the chair out as she sat, and helped her pull it in.

"So, where are we?"

He walked around the table to sit opposite her, "that depends on your perspective."

She frowned, or more realistically glared until he elaborated.

"We're still in the house, but this part of the house is now somewhere else."

"Where else?"

He looked around him, "at a guess, I'd say the Plaza Hotel, somewhere around 1910."

"That's quite a specific guess."

"Well, the Plaza opened in 1907, the new carpet smell has gone, and is showing a little wear."

She snorted, "how do you know this is the Plaza, and that it opened in 1907?"

"I was here."

Morag opened her mouth. And then she shut it.

Again, she opened, and after a beat, closed her mouth.

There were too many questions related to those statements.

Then, "how could you have been at the Plaza, let's see..." she did a quick calculation, "111 years ago." She looked him up and down, "and about 80 years before you were born?"

He looked embarrassed, "let's just say there was an incident I'd really rather not go into right now. Can we talk about that later?"

She glared at him a little longer, and when he didn't seem inclined to say anything further, reluctantly nodded.

"Shall we have some dinner then?"

She nodded again.

He beckoned, and a tuxedo-clad waiter seemingly appeared from nowhere. He flicked a napkin open and lay it in her lap, and did the same for the Young Master.

The Young Master gave him a set of instructions in what seemed to be fluent French, so it seemed obvious they weren't in an Australian hotel.

The waiter nodded, removed some of the cutlery, and walked away.

Curious that his bedroom moved independently of the house in time *and* space.

Not that anyone would believe her.

She wouldn't have believed it herself except that she was sitting there, inside Hayward Hall. She checked behind her to see the door was still there.

And however unlikely, she was somewhere else as well.

"Paris?" she asked.

"New York."

"Can I go outside and see?"

"Best not without me." He checked his watch, "we only have a couple of hours here, and you can't be late."

"Young Master..." she growled a little in frustration, "must I keep calling you Young Master, or can I call you by your name?"

"Henry," he smiled, "my name is Henry Fox."

"So, Henry..."

The waiter brought a bottle of white wine, and she stopped talking to watch the proceedings. The waiter showed Henry the label, and he nodded. The waiter removed the cork with a small pop and poured a little in the glass in front of Henry.

He swilled it around the glass, sniffed it, tasted it, then nodded. The waiter poured her a glass, topped up Henry's, then took the bottle away with him.

Morag sipped her wine, holding a little in her mouth to appreciate the crisp dry taste while the waiter cleared away the extra glasses.

"Henry—."

"Morag, I know you want answers, and I'd like to give them to you, but let's look at tonight as a kind of job interview.

"If I like you, you can stay. And if you like me, you can choose to stay.

"And in a day or two, if we agree you're to stay, then I will answer all your questions.

"Does that sound fair?"

However unfair that seemed, he'd effectively reminded her he was her boss and not her date.

She shifted in her seat; of course, she didn't need to know anything more than he was prepared to tell her.

And of course, she wouldn't need to know anything unless he was employing her.

Feeling as though she was being put in her place, she nodded, "deal."

He smiled and held up his glass, "then, cheers."

She tapped it with hers, "cheers."

They drank.

And then sat in awkward silence.

Henry asked, "read any good books lately," at the same time Morag asked, "do you watch movies?"

They laughed for a moment, and he said, "go ahead."

"No, you go first."

"Ah, okay, well I was asking if you'd read any books."

She sipped her wine before she replied, "I'm not much of a reader at the moment, I'm usually too tired."

"Ah, that's a shame. I read the latest Epiphany Bombshell political thriller. It was intense."

"Was it? Perhaps you could lend it to me. If we agree on the contract, I won't be working nights anymore."

"I'll do that," he said.

"I usually watch movies," she said, "you tend to get more story in less time."

The waiter arrived, with two plates of shells covered in a green sauce, setting one before each of them. "Oysters Rockefeller," he said in heavily accented English, "*bon appétit*".

Morag bent to smell the dish before lifting a fork, "are you trying to wow me with your luxurious dinner then?"

He watched as she spooned one into her mouth, "not really. Oysters are common and cheap in this time."

"Oh, my goodness, that's good," she said, licking her lips.

He grunted in agreement but didn't stop to talk.

"Sorry," he said when he'd finished, "I didn't realise how hungry I was."

She was still trying to fork up the dressing that had spilt onto her plate, "umm, there's celery, and perhaps chives." She tutted for a moment, "capers, parsley, and some kind of alcohol." She smacked her lips, "I'm pretty sure I could approximate this."

"I'm sure you could. What were you saying?"

She frowned, "I've forgotten. No, wait, movies. I like books, but movies are quicker."

"What's your favourite then."

"I like fantasy and science fiction, but romantic comedies are easy to digest."

"Not mystery or suspense?"

"I'm not sure they're a thing these days, though I liked *Rear Window*."

The waiter returned to take the remains of the oysters away, along with the wine glasses.

Neither said anything.

The waiter came back with a bottle of red wine, letting Henry taste and approve the wine before he served it to her. Once more he left with the bottle.

She saluted him and sipped the rich, room temperature wine. "This is tasty. How do you come to know so much about wine?"

He sprawled a little in his seat, "in the old days when I was a child, Hayward Hall was always full of guests because my parents entertained a lot. It was quite a ways out of town in those days, and they had giant house parties. The wine stocks in Australia were quite limited so we travelled to Europe on buying expeditions. And then as time went by, my father wrote to the vineyards and replenished our stocks every year."

"May I know when that was?"

Henry looked at her for a while and was about to speak when the waiter arrived with the next course.

"Minted lamb, new potatoes and garden peas." He set the plates in front of them, and a small jug of gravy between them.

Morag held the edges of her seat, trying not to say or do anything that would distract him.

Henry picked up his fork and moved a few peas around the plate.

He sighed.

"1880."

Morag felt the floor falling away from her, and was glad she had a death grip on the seat.

"1880," she repeated. "Then you're at least... Twenty, twenty... 140 years old!"

He smiled a flat smile, "I was born in 1876, so 144 years to be exact."

"That's horrific!

"Damn it, that's not what I meant." She tried to think of a way to rephrase it to express exactly what she was feeling. "I mean, like," she waved her hands to suggest something more, "I'd go nuts being alive so long. How do you manage to keep going?"

He threw the wine down his throat, and beckoned for the waiter, "I don't have a choice."

Morag gulped her own wine, half horrified by the idea of living so long herself, half horrified for Henry's parents who had lost him to whatever hell he lived in, and half horrified that Henry had no one left who knew or cared about him.

That was too many halves for anyone.

They watched the waiter pour more wine into Henry's glass, and then hers, "leave it," he said, and the waiter backed away.

He savagely cut into his lamb and shovelled it into his mouth.

She watched and waited as he chewed.

"It's like that movie *Groundhog Day*," he said, cutting another slice of lamb, "except every day is different. I wake up, I walk out the door and start the day in another place and time.

"If I try to go back through the door into the house, I wake up the next day. If I die, I wake up the next day. If I stay up past midnight, I wake up the next day

"With whatever's the equivalent of the two quid I had in my pocket that last day in the house."

Morag took another gulp from her wineglass and clamped her spare hand between her thighs to stop herself from reaching out to him.

"That must be hard."

He grimaced, "like my mother used to say, what can't be cured, must be endured."

"But isn't there some way to fix this?"

"I'm not exactly sure what happened, so I don't know where to start fixing it."

"But with the resources of the universe at your disposal, you could go anywhere, and try anything!"

"For 24 hours only."

She scratched her head, then shook it.

What kind of sissy was he to live every day for a hundred years and not try to find a way out?

She did some more calculations in her head, "if you'd spent just two hours a day, every day, you'd have more than 60,000 hours worth of knowledge."

"I'm just trying to live a normal life, one day at a time, as best I can."

"So you haven't done anything, or learned anything that might be useful towards getting you out of here?"

"What's the point? It is what it is."

"And yet at least once, you tried to kill yourself to get out of here."

He sighed, and put down his cutlery, "I think you should go now. I think you should pack your suitcase and leave Hayward Hall."

"I—"

He stood up so abruptly his chair fell back on the carpet with a dull thud.

"You should leave."

"But—"

"GO."

And as she walked out the door, he slammed it behind her.

She tried to open it, but it wouldn't budge.

She looked at her watch; eleven o'clock.

Where had the time gone?

The house was in almost complete darkness, just a dim glow rising up the stairwell from the kitchen.

And the house was still, and utterly silent.

No rodents, no creaking as the house contracted in the cool evening air. No sign of owls, or possums, or other nocturnal creatures.

Morag was angry.

It seemed Henry had lost hope.

And she was defeated, fired before she'd even started, and with debts piling up.

She needed this job. It was the only thing the agency had offered her.

And she had no intention of leaving the Hall.

No intention of leaving him to his misery.

Her shoulders had ridden up without her noticing, so she forcibly dropped them.

She was here as a housekeeper, and keep the house was exactly what she planned to do.

Despite the skin crawling on the back of her neck, she didn't turn to look at the Master Bedroom come hotel dining room.

Just pulled out her phone, and used its light to guide her.

Turning the light on at the top of the stairs, she descended to the ground level and did a circuit of the rooms; shutting the front door, and making sure all the windows were secure before returning to the top floor to her bedroom.

She knew next to nothing about the incident that had sent flying in time and space, but she'd passed through a library, and a study, and chances were that the household records were kept in one or both of those.

And they were as good a place to start as any.

Back in her own room, she pulled out a journal to record her day. And as she started writing about Henry's dilemma, it occurred to her to wonder whether he kept records of his days.

He seemed to know a lot about the New York hotel, did he know as much about the other places he visited?

Perhaps there was some kind of pattern to when and where he landed.

If his pockets reset to two pounds every day, then if he kept a journal it would probably disappear every day. But if she was in the house...

Perhaps she could pass him a new journal each day, and maybe, just maybe the journal would appear in her room the next morning.

And perhaps it might not reset to a blank journal. Perhaps what he'd written that day would be there when she woke up in the morning?

And if it wasn't?

Maybe she could set up a mini-office outside his door and scan the records into a PC. And perhaps because they were in the house, they wouldn't disappear.

So the important thing for the morning was to explain her ideas to him and get him to at least try them out.

So where would he be in the morning?

And would it be a good place to start his research?

When she woke in the morning, she felt weirdly refreshed and raring to go. It might take a long time to do the research, and she wanted to get started as soon as possible.

But first, she had to make Henry breakfast and serve it at 9 am.

With no idea what he might want.

There was nothing in the pantry to suggest what he usually ate.

When she went on holidays, she usually tried to eat an enormous breakfast. Something that would keep her going perhaps as far as dinner. Though Henry's lunch was to be served at noon.

She made three bacon and egg rolls; two for Henry, and one for her. A thermos of coffee with two mugs, with a side of paper and a pen.

Standing before the door, she experienced a moment of nervousness but quashed it down.

He did not invite her to come in, so she boldly knocked on the door.

And after a few moments when he had not answered it, she knocked again, "Henry?"

Still nothing, so she opened it.

How interesting, he couldn't lock the door. He must have been standing with his back to it to hold it shut.

She allowed herself a grin as she looked onto a broad meadow filled with grasses and wildflowers, waving in a slight breeze. Birds called and swooped in the distance.

The day was on the cool side, and she wondered would he have warm enough clothes. That would make a grand experiment.

"Henry?" she called again, "Hello Henry?"

There was no reply.

"Henry, come out. I need to talk to you."

Still nothing.

"Will I take your breakfast away with me? It's bacon and egg rolls."

The sound of a body moving through the grass made her turn, though of course, she couldn't see through the door to the other side.

"Henry?"

He walked around the door, dressed as she was, in blue jeans and a blue striped t-shirt that were so nondescript they could have belonged any time in the last hundred years. And what looked to be the same brown brogues, "yes it's me. You said there something about bacon?"

It seemed ridiculous, but she asked anyway, "may I come in?"

And equally ridiculously, smiling at the idea, he gestured a welcome.

She stepped over the threshold, and offered the tray she was carrying towards him. He took a roll and started eating while she knelt, still holding the tray, and lay it on the ground.

"I hope you don't mind, I brought enough for two."

He nodded, and she poured two cups of sweet milky coffee before picking up her roll.

He sat, and they ate in a more or less companionable silence.

When he finished his first roll, he said, "I'm sorry for snapping at you last night."

"And I'm sorry for nagging you, I'm sure you've tried researching."

"I have, but you might have a new perspective, and I should at least hear you out," he picked up one of the coffees and took a sip.

"As a matter of fact," she said dusting off her hands and pickup up her coffee, "I do have an idea how we might progress the research."

"I'm all ears."

"Have you tried keeping a journal?"

"No."

She grinned, "I'd like to try an experiment, and this looks like a good day to try it out."

She outlined her ideas about the journal.

"It's not a bad plan. I've never woken up with anything other than the cash with me, but I've also never tried passing goods back and forth through the door.

Let's do a couple of small-scale experiments now, and move on from there."

"What did you have in mind?"

He wrote something on a page, folded it into an aeroplane, and flew it through the door, "fetch," he said.

She rolled her eyes at him, and scrambled up and through the door. She unfolded the paper and showed him that the writing was still there.

"That's a positive sign," he said.

"Then I'll order the computer equipment," she said pulling out her phone and taking notes on it, "and see if I can get an express delivery—"

"What's that you have there?" Henry asked.

"My phone?" she looked blankly at him for a moment, "ah, you might not have understood them. It's kind of a machine, you can take notes, make phone calls, send texts."

"Can I see it?" he asked with an avaricious gleam in his eyes.

She dropped the paper back in the corridor and walked back to him. "I'm not sure it will work here," she said handing it over.

He turned it over and over in his hands, tapped a few buttons, and then dropped it in surprise when one of them was her music.

She scooped it up and turned it off.

"I think I want one of these too."

"It would certainly help, and I can order one for you, but I think maybe we should experiment with the paper first. In case it doesn't reset back to me."

"Sensible. But order one for me anyway, I can hand it back to you in the evening."

"Sure. Now, do you want me to bring you lunch at your usual time?"

"No, it's more important you get organised, and there's a town on the door side anyway." he reached into his pocket and counted out the contents, "and I have \$120 at my disposal."

He looked at her, trying to gauge its adequacy.

"Sounds like you might be within a few decades of my time, and that ought to get you lunch with some left over."

"Fine," he said, getting to his feet, "meet you back here at 8?"

"Sure," she grinned at him, delighted that he was giving her the go-ahead, "in the meantime, why don't' you try to catalogue as much as you can remember of the last few days for me?"

"Okay," he squatted to fold the paper and pen into his pocket, then scooped up the last bacon roll.

"Ah. Keep the receipts for an expense claim against the estate accounts. Yvonne should have left some forms to sign giving you authority over the bank accounts, so once you've done that so you can use them."

"Cool," she said, shoving the phone into her back pocket.

He turned and started to walk away.

"Hey," she called out, "do you mind if I leave the tray here? To see what happens to it?"

He turned his head to look back at her, "sure. What's the worst that can happen?"

"Right," she said, dusting her hands together and turning towards him, "Now then. What was the date of the incident that started this?

"I'm not sure how that's relevant."

"Ah. I watched a show where some guy went travelling in time, and there was some kind of coinciding astrological and weather event."

He shrugged, "okay then, 9th of September 1904."

She made a note on her phone, "great, see you at dinner then!"

He waved and kept walking.

Back in the house, it seemed as though she ought to at least do a little light dusting. That was what she'd been employed for after all.

But making a start on the Henry Project seemed a better idea.

And more fun.

She called a cab and took a ride to the closest large shopping precinct.

First stop the bank to sort out the accounts and order a credit card - she had no idea how long it would be until she could get him out of there, and it would be much more convenient to order goods to be delivered than go out to get them.

Then she visited a computer store and paid over the odds to get laptops, printers and scanners delivered to the house that afternoon.

She organised the phone and took that with her.

Then a bunch of notebooks and pens; a different colour for each day of the week. Thinking positively that if they used a book for each day of the week, any patterns would show up more easily.

Morag's footsteps slowed as she approached a Chinese restaurant, and smelled something tasty. She was so tempted to stop by for some tea and dumplings, but knowing she had a delivery due in a few hours made her speed up again.

But the lingering odour of chilli, garlic and onions was so delicious she turned around and ordered a serve of garlic chicken to take away.

Henry's plight was urgent, but she couldn't serve him well if she didn't take care of herself.

Back in the house, lunch consumed, she decided to set up the office because it had a fine view along the drive and the office was clearly next to the entry foyer for that reason.

Besides which, the household records were more likely to be in that space. And she might have time to look at some of them while she waited.

She looked in the ground floor store and retrieved an ancient barrel vacuum cleaner and some feather dusters that had stood the test of time.

More or less.

She opened the curtains, displacing more dust, and regretting her lack of a face mask.

Undeterred, she pulled her t-shirt up to cover her nose and opened the window as far as it would go.

The vacuum still worked, which made her wonder about the safety of the wiring, but it was heavy and difficult to manoeuvre.

Thank goodness she'd bought a surge protector and a backup battery to put between the computer equipment and the wall.

She swished the duster around in her left hand, and holding the suction pipe in her right, vacuumed the air first, and the curtains second.

She tried out the black Bakelite phone, and of course, it wasn't connected. She followed the lead back to the wall, to find the plug was like something she'd seen in a museum. That whole thing would need to be replaced.

She emptied the vacuum out the window, then vacuumed the carpet.

Which turned out to be blue with a yellow pattern that reminded her of the upstairs wallpaper. Had they commissioned carpet and wallpaper to match?

Hopefully, given the room was the only one with a phone line, and was located close to the front of the house, it would be easy to install a base station with handsets that would have sufficient range to get through the house.

She emptied the vacuum out the window once more, before returning the vacuum and dusters to the store, then filled a bucket with water and took it with some rags back to the office to wipe the surface down.

And wondered if she dared hire a squad of cleaners for a week or so to get the house thoroughly cleaned.

Would the house stand up to it?

Something to consider for another time.

With the office in a mostly usable condition, she went back upstairs to get her journal, then out into the garden to find a spot with phone coverage.

Which turned out to be right outside the door, so maybe it was just that the walls were old and thick, and well built.

Nonetheless, she'd need to get the internet connected up to the house, so she called her phone company and arranged a connection. The company had a cancellation and could come the next day.

She crossed her fingers that the power would be good enough for that too.

And then she sat in the shade of a tree and did some internet searches.

Within half an hour she'd discovered the 9th of September was indeed a good candidate for fantastical events:

- There had been a solar eclipse, and
- A low atmospheric pressure trough leading to unsettled weather, and
- An Antarctic disturbance had moved into the Bight.

All of which seemed an excellent indication that something significant had occurred on the day.

A little further investigation revealed the eclipse was part of two different series:

- The Saros cycle, next due the 25th of November 2030, and
- The Inex cycle, next due 31st May 2049.

Either of which was an unfortunately long time away.

Henry would surely be discouraged.

So that just meant that she had to keep him occupied with finding out how to reverse the effect.

And of course, time inside the Master Bedroom moved to its own drum.

And she'd be right outside, doing what she could to assist.

Or maybe she wouldn't tell him about the eclipses just yet.

《《 • 》》

Later that evening, washed and dressed in clean jeans and a long-sleeved shirt, she stood outside the door.

By this point, she'd hoped to have achieved a bit more.

But the laptop sat on a table she'd dragged from another room and set up on the corner of the wall, next to the door, partly blocking the corridor so she could take notes if she needed to. It was connected to a printer and a scanner in case she needed to make copies of anything.

Plus, she'd stacked all the journals and a bunch of other stationery in the hope that should it disappear during his night, it would reappear on the table.

Opposite the door, she'd set up an incident board, like you see in crime shows, where she could keep him up to date on her investigations. Currently showing the page he'd given her that morning.

She'd set up an email account for him, and downloaded a bunch of apps that might be useful to his phone. The hard part might be teaching him how to use the phone.

She rolled her neck against her shoulders, then linked her fingers together, turning her palms outward, and stretched side to side, forward and backwards, and knocked on the door before she was ready.

He opened it just as she was turning away to stretch her back.

"You're back!" he said.

She turned back to face him, "my front!" she said, and he snorted.

He was inside a pub.

"Ah, so the door turns up wherever you are," she said, "that's good to know."

He grinned and stood back so she could see.

It might have been a themed pub, or it might have been an actual British pub.

It wasn't that different to one she'd visited in London called the Nag's Head, with worn wooden floors, chipped and dented tables and chairs, and of course darts boards at the end of the bar.

The air was fragrant with beer, steak and chips, and a hint of mayonnaise. The sound of muted conversation suggested the pub was half full.

She stepped back to show him her incident room styling, hoping it would look suitably futuristic and full of potential.

He seemed suitably impressed, but he could tell something about her was off.

"Look," he said, "come in and we'll order, then you can tell me what's bugging you."

She chose steak and chips with salad and beer, and Henry ordered the same. They took a number and brought it back to their table.

The beer when it arrived was warm, which if nothing else confirmed the geographical exactness of the British pub.

"So, what's up?"

She pulled out her journal and looked at his hopeful, yet puzzled face.

She couldn't lie to him.

So, she relayed the findings of the day's researches.

He surprised her, "that's fantastic! This is great news - you're hired!"

She looked at his radiant face, wondering if he'd finally gone mad.

"I'm sorry? I'm hired?"

He took a swig of his beer, and nudged hers closer to her, "yes, you're hired."

"I'm hired?" she repeated, "I don't understand."

He grinned, "24 hours ago I was telling you to get lost. I didn't know anything about the situation I find myself in. And today I know there may have been two sets of cosmic influences."

"But it might be decades before you can live a normal life."

"Ah, but I live in a time machine, and if you take the job, I've got you on the outside."

"But I haven't done anything that no one else could do."

A cheerful waitress came through and left their meals, and after being reassured they weren't expecting anything else, taking the number away with her.

He picked a chip off his plate, sucking the air through his mouth to cool it before he could chew it.

"No one bothered until you."

She speared a bit of salad and chewed.

It was true she needed a job. And this was the kind of job could make a significant difference in the life of her employer.

Furthermore, her new boss wouldn't be under her feet micromanaging all day.

"All right, I'll take it."

He jumped up and gave her a spontaneous kiss on each cheek, "that's the best news I've heard since five minutes ago!"

«« • »»

It was the November 25 2030, and Morag'd been working at Hayward Hall for almost a decade.

She stood outside the Master Bedroom door, listening intently to the sounds within.

If their calculations were correct, at 11:57 she would be able to enter the Master Bedroom at the time

Henry had detonated the device that sent him spinning through space and time.

She stood, her eyes fastened on the GPS linked watch on her left wrist showing the exact time, and the other hand on the doorknob.

Counting down.

Henry had described the situation, so she knew what she was looking for.

At exactly 11:57, she threw the door open, sprinted across the bedroom and slapped the device from his hand.

"What the devil do you think you're doing?" he demanded.

"I'm saving you from yourself."

The device detonated with a flash, and she covered him from the fallout with her body.

The light got brighter and brighter, and she had to close her eyes against the glare.

But she was jubilant. She had saved him.

She would wake up the next morning in her bed, and he would wake in his.

Job done.

THE END

LOVE IN THE PAST TENSE

With next to no noise, Roberts, his father's valet, eased the bedroom door open and brought in a cup of tea.

"Good morning Young Master Henry." He sat the cup on the bedside table before opening the curtains to let the dull sunlight stream in on the mostly awake Master Fox.

Henry Fox had inherited Hayward Hall when his father died suddenly some six months before, and he, as well as the servants, were having a hard time adjusting to his new station in life.

Surely 28 years old was sufficiently old to not feel like a child dressing up.

He sat up, waved the shamefaced valet away to the dressing room and reached for the tea. Giving it an unnecessary stir with the silver spoon, he took a sip and looked through the large windows, out over the formal gardens. Partially obscured by the rain.

They were nice enough, though a little old fashioned; he'd have to do something about that at some point.

But he missed his father enough to not want to mess with anything just yet, and besides, he knew it would upset his mother. After all, the garden was an act of love for her.

She walked the paths every day. Often with Miss Viola Seagrove in attendance.

What he could do though, was get rid of some of this monstrous mahogany furniture and oppressively dark, striped wallpaper.

Or perhaps it could wait until he married. To the ubiquitous Miss Seagrove

Who would no doubt have an Opinion about what should replace it.

He sighed.

Conveniently she was staying at the house, ostensibly as a companion to his mother, but presumably, their goal was to ensure she became his wife.

His mother adored her, and he didn't actively dislike her, so he'd been prepared to go with the flow for his mother's sake.

It wasn't as if they would be joined at the hip forever after.

He sighed once more, drank the rest of his tea, then heaved himself out of the bed, and into the day.

As he took care of his ablutions in the bathroom, he blessed his father's foresight for including plumbed in bathrooms in the house design. Controversial at the time, but damned convenient now.

Moving into the Master bedroom had been worth it just for the attached bath and dressing rooms. Not to mention not having to share with his brothers.

Roberts, presented a fashionable black pinstriped wool morning suit, with a contrasting blue patterned vest. Paired with a white Arundel collar shirt, black silk bow tie, and the peacock feather patterned braces embroidered by his mother.

In a small act of rebellion, he chose the brown oxfords instead of black.

Roberts smoothed the suit over his shoulders and brushed it out while Henry threaded the bar of his father's watch through his waistcoat.

Watch in his right waistcoat pocket, penknife in his left, and adjusted the fall of the locket fob.

He flicked open the locket to see the photograph of his mother on the left, and himself as a baby on the right. It was something he'd seen his father do countless times when faced with a big decision.

He'd hoped one day to replace his photograph with his wife's, but couldn't quite imagine Miss Seagrove's face in place, smiling slightly back at him like his mother.

He snapped the locket shut, grimaced at himself in the mirror for a moment and smoothed the hair on his head and moustache once last time.

Ideally, he'd like the kind of love match his parents had shared. But he couldn't imagine sharing that intense closeness with anyone. Not anyone he knew, and certainly not Miss "call me Viola" Seagrove.

Turning away, before straightening his shoulders and leaving to do battle in the dining room.

He could get breakfast in his room but didn't want to trouble the servants. They had enough dealing with his mother.

The dining room was also full of monstrous mahogany furniture, though the vine patterned wallpaper was less oppressive.

As the house was still in mourning, the extra chairs and dining table leaves were packed away leaving a more intimate setting for just the family.

"Good Morning," he said as he entered the room.

Four of his brothers were arguing with two of his sisters, and they interrupted their quarrelling for long enough to return his greeting.

His mother was trying unsuccessfully to referee.

Knowing the other three were making Nanny's life hell somewhere else in the house made it almost bearable.

"And how are you this fine morning," Miss Seagrove simpered.

Henry grunted and collected his choice of break-fast items from the buffet. The mahogany buffet.

He rolled his eyes at the wall.

At both the buffet and Miss Seagrove.

She had snagged the seat next to the head of the table, so he had to either sit next to her or demote himself, neither of the options particularly appealing.

He shook out the day's *The Argus* newspaper, September 9th, 1904.

He didn't have to feign interest in an article about the day's solar eclipse while shovelling breakfast into his mouth.

Miss Seagrove didn't take the hint, "you seem a little peaky, have you perhaps been drinking a little too much whisky?"

Henry grunted and raised the newspaper a little so she couldn't see him over it.

Wasn't she perhaps taking somewhat of a liberty with the intimacy afforded by his mother?

He flipped over to the weather, "Freshening northern winds, gradually becoming unsettled."

It was already unsettled here, and he was going to give himself indigestion the speed with which he was eating.

"Would you consider joining your mother and me for a walk in the garden after breakfast?"

He grunted again.

On second thoughts, he wasn't sure he could go with the flow. He was starting to dislike her.

Why did he think he needed to marry her again?

"I'm quite sure it would do you the world of good."

He folded the newspaper, placed his cutlery side by side on his plate, and sculled his tea.

"I really don't think so Miss Seagrove, I must organise my speech notes.

He sketched a quick incline of his shoulders in her direction before she could say *Please, call me Viola,* and almost sprinted from the dining room.

Dammit, he left the newspaper behind.

Back in his room, he looked out the window.

He couldn't go to the library as he'd be fair game for the rest of his family.

And the study held too many memories of his father.

But he didn't really want to spend the day skulking in his bedroom.

He was about to open his pocket watch when a woman threw the door open.

At least he thought it was a woman.

She had short red hair and appeared to be wearing some kind of figure-hugging swimsuit.

She ran across the room and slapped the watch from his hand.

"What the devil do you think you're doing?" he demanded.

"I'm saving you from yourself."

She threw herself in his arms, crashing into his body. He took a step back to stabilise his stance, but distracted by her floral fragrance, couldn't correct sufficiently to prevent them from falling to the floor.

She was incredibly heavy.

And wasn't wearing a corset.

"Er, Miss?"

She didn't respond.

He shook her arm, and she didn't respond.

"Miss?"

Oh, that was just fabulous.

She'd passed out.

He lay on the floor, thinking if he was dreaming, it wasn't such a bad dream. A Bathing Beauty saving him from himself.

Roberts chose that moment to enter the bedroom, then turned to go.

"Wait," Henry said.

Roberts turned his body, but not his face towards his employer.

"Er, yes Mr Fox?"

"You can see her, right?"

"Of course, how could I not see a half-naked woman in your bedroom?"

Henry let out a sigh of relief, "that's excellent, I'm not imagining it. Would you help me get her to the bed?"

Roberts lifted her shoulders, allowing Henry to wriggle out from underneath her, and together they managed to carry her to his bed.

"What now?" Henry asked.

Roberts looked at him, and after a beat, said, "you're the boss."

"Oh, right.

"I suppose we should find somewhere for her to stay. Should it be servants or guests?" Henry looked at the valet.

Roberts didn't say anything.

Henry looked at him some more.

"The Blue Bedroom by the stairs is currently un-occupied, I'll ask one of the maids do it up."

"Good."

Roberts left the room.

Henry dragged a chair over to the bed and watched her.

She was quite pale, with dark shadows under her eyes.

He wondered how she'd got into the house, and up the stairs without anyone raising the alarm.

And for that matter, where had she come from that no one between there and here had batted an eyelid.

That she'd lost her hair suggested hospital - the closest was The Alfred Hospital. Could she have walked for an hour to get here?

Not in that get-up.

Or had she somehow escaped from the Point Nepean Quarantine Station? But that would have taken days, and she seemed too fresh for that.

It was as if she'd bathed just before opening his door.

He wanted to keep her to himself, and not tell anyone, but at the very least she'd need some proper clothes.

If he could just get a moment alone with his mother.

He took a walk around the verandas of the house so he could look in through the windows of the main buildings to find out where she was, and if she was alone.

As he walked along the West verandah, he saw her in the Drawing Room, embroidering something.

Alone.

So he opened the glass doors and walked in.

"Hello Mother," he bent to kiss her cheek before sitting beside her.

She continued her embroidery, "shall I ring for some tea?"

"There's no need."

"Nonsense," she picked up a small bell from the table beside her and rang it. Almost immediately the newest maid bounded in and, almost as soon was on her way again.

Mrs Fox took up her embroidery again, "now, what's this about son?"

"A young woman broke into my bedroom this morning, and then fell unconscious."

"That's interesting. Where did she come from? And how did she get here?"

"I can't say, though her hair's been cut short, and she's wearing some kind of swimsuit."

"The Yarra Bend Lunatic Asylum I should think," Miss Seagrove said entering the room.

He stood politely, but quickly sat back down, next to his mother, forcing Miss Seagrove to an armchair.

"Perhaps Barnes could make some enquiries," Mrs Fox said, "in the meantime, where will you put her?"

"I'm having the Blue Room made up."

Miss Seagrove hissed, and Mrs Fox and Henry glanced at each other before looking at her.

She shrugged, "I'm not sure the bedroom opposite you is appropriate. Wouldn't it be better to put her in a maid's room at the back of the house?"

Henry for one wasn't having it, "we don't know anything about this woman, she needs to be where I can keep an eye on her."

"That's right Viola," his mother agreed, "Henry can keep us safe if she turns out to be a threat of some kind."

"Mother, I'll need you to arrange some clothing for her, and perhaps someone to take care of her until she wakes up and we know more."

"I can do that," Miss Seagrove said, I want to protect you from walk-in gold diggers."

When Mrs Fox said, "that's a good idea," Henry looked at her aghast, but her face remained inscrutable.

As Miss Seagrove preened, Henry wondered whether his mother was finally feeling the strain of Miss Seagrove's constant presence.

In the meantime, he had little option but to leave the stranger to her "tender" ministrations.

«« • »»

Morag woke suddenly.

She lay awake, eyes closed, trying to figure out what had woken her. Something about Hayward Hall was different.

For one thing, the room smelled as though a female had just exited it, and given she lived alone, that was disconcerting.

To compound matters, she could hear the murmur of conversation, though she couldn't tell how far away it was. Or whether she'd left a television on in the other room.

Additionally, there was something not quite right about the light. In her room, the light and slight breeze from the open window came from her left, and in this room, from the foot of the bed.

She risked opening her eyes.

She was alone.

Looking across a nicer carved bed than her usual one, to a window with a view over a carefully manicured forest instead of over lawn to the stables.

Aside from the bed, there was an old-fashioned matching armoire, chest of drawers and dressing table, as well as a bedside cabinet and chair.

She realised she was in the Blue Room, though the carpet and wallpaper were way more vivid and colourful than in her time.

As you'd expect when you'd travelled 116 years into the past.

She knew there was a toilet behind the stairs, so she struggled out from the covers.

After taking a moment to comprehend, then bunch up the voluminous nightgown someone had put her in, she cautiously opened the door to make sure no one was nearby and scampered down the corridor.

How long had she been out of it?

Long enough for the weather to start warming up.

She washed her hands, bunched up the nightgown and snuck back up the corridor.

Instead of heading around the corner to the room she'd woken up in, she headed across to Henry's room.

She opened the door long enough to check that he was there, but this time, gave herself a moment to fully appreciate how well he looked, here in his element.

Without the strain of hopping from time to time for more than a century, he seemed younger, though she supposed that technically he was.

He might have been wearing the same clothes as the last time she'd seen him, but there was something subtly different about the way this Henry styled his hair to future Henry's styling. He had the same ordinary brown hair and eyes, though the moustache was new to her.

It suited him.

She opened the door fully, and as he looked up to see who was there, she raced across the room to embrace him, "oh Henry, thank goodness you're here. It really worked! You're safe in your own time!"

He tried to disentangle her, "I'm sure I have no idea what you're talking about."

She took a step back to look at him again, trying to pin down what the difference was. "I can't get over how well you look in this time."

She went to embrace him again, but he held her shoulders to stop her from approaching any closer.

"Miss...

"I don't know who you are, or how you know me, or why you feel the need to be so familiar, but I would appreciate it if you would take a step back and explain yourself."

She took a step back, slapped her palm against her forehead, "of course! I forgot you don't know me in this time. I'm Morag Clementine, I'm your future housekeeper, we know each other in the future."

Henry took a few steps back and carefully sat down in a chair, looking at her like she'd escaped from the lunatic asylum.

"Miss Clementine, do you have any idea how ridiculous you sound right now?"

She crossed the room and threw herself on his bed.

He winced.

"Well, I suppose I wouldn't believe me either, but I brought proof. Do you know where my clothes are?"

"Your swimsuit has been laundered and placed in your room, as has some proper clothing. Can you guess what I would prefer you to wear?"

Her swimsuit?

Ah, for some reason she hadn't considered that jungle print leggings and matching tank top might not be the most appropriate clothing to wear.

He ran a finger underneath his collar, and it occurred to her that lying on his bed, naked under her gown, might be doing things to him.

"There's a certain kind of woman who entertains gentleman in bed chambers, and I can only restrain myself so far from taking advantage of the situation.

"Perhaps you could do something about putting some proper clothes on sooner rather than later."

Morag laughed, "I wouldn't have put you down as quite so prim and—"

A young woman threw the door open without so much as a tap at the door, and Henry stood up, "Miss Seagrove, what do you mean by this?"

The woman blushed and took a step back, "I apologise. That woman escaped the bedroom while I was refreshing myself. I assume she made a beeline to your room."

Henry's eyes flicked across to her, and the woman's eyes followed his.

"Oh my goodness, there you are, you little tramp!" She advanced across the room seemingly determined to wrestle her from the bed and out the room.

Morag scrambled backwards on the bed.

"Miss Seagrove," Henry roared.

She stopped and looked over her shoulder at him.

"Can you not see we were having a conversation?"

She drew herself up to her full uptight height, "I do not think it is appropriate for you to interview this woman in her present state of undress. Please allow me to dress her, and continue your conversation somewhere more public, like the Drawing Room, or the Sitting Room."

Morag didn't know what the fuss was about, but when Henry crumpled, it seemed Miss Seagrove had won that round.

He nodded.

Miss Seagrove grabbed her arm with a vice-like grip and dragged her back to the Blue Room.

"You are utterly shameless," Miss Seagrove told her as she helped Morag don a white chemise and drawers.

She handed Morag stockings and cute lace-up boots, frowning as she paced the room while she waited for Morag to get them on.

"Mr Fox is my fiancé," she said as she pulled the corset's lacing tighter than Morag thought was necessary, and her heart plummeted.

Henry hadn't mentioned a fiancé, and she'd assumed they would pick up where they'd left off.

But, Miss Seagrove was there first, and she could only assume his feelings for the woman were genuine.

She would have to back off.

Miss Seagrove picked up a petticoat, "I would appreciate you keeping your distance." She dragged it over Morag's head, "in fact, the sooner you give up whatever your game is," she held out a flaring frilled navy-blue skirt for Morag to step into, "the better."

She handed Morag a white long-sleeved blouse ruffled on the front and sleeves, then did the buttons on the back up.

Miss Seagrove nodded at her, "and that's how ladies dress, not out in their swimsuits walking the town."

"Oh!"

Morag started opening and closing the drawers looking for the leggings and top.

Or more particularly the locket she'd been wearing when she'd arrived.

"Looking for this?" Miss Seagrove said, letting the necklace dangle from her fingers. "I'm keeping it for now, you can take it back when you leave."

Morag guessed she hadn't opened the locket to see the picture of her and Henry that night in Shanghai. Then again, the locket was a puzzle locket they'd bought there, so it was unlikely she'd be able to open it anyway.

All she had to do, was steal it back.

Miss Seagrove deposited her in the Drawing Room without asking her if she wanted anything to eat.

Rude.

She looked around the cosy room. A piano at one end for night time entertainments, conversational seating with small tables loaded with photos and knickknacks where it would be almost impossible to set your drinks.

Light streamed through the windows and glass doors.

On a day as beautiful as today, she would've opened the doors to let the smell of the rose garden in.

And seeing as no one was there, and she'd been left to her own devices, she walked across the room noting a hidden coffee table holding some embroidery.

She folded the doors open and stepped outside unto the verandah.

Morag was about to take a step down into the garden when a small, well-fed pug arrived.

She bent down to let it sniff her hand, then scratched its head. "You are a darling, aren't you?" she asked it. It didn't reply, though a male voice from above her did, "Dante is indeed a darling."

Henry held out his hand to pull her to her feet, "I see you are now dressed appropriately for your conditions," and he held her hand for longer than was strictly necessary.

Remembering he was someone else's husband to be, she pulled her hand back, held her arms out, and spun around once, "how do you like me now?" she asked.

"Well," he looked her up and down, and she had the feeling that this outfit was sexier than the nightgown she'd worn earlier. "You look fit for decent company at any rate."

Morag smiled ruefully back at him, "I hadn't really thought very much about what would happen when I got here."

Morag's stomach growled, and she rubbed it.

Henry laid a hand on her arm, warm through the thin fabric of her blouse, giving her the jitters. "Have you eaten yet, are you hungry?"

"I am a bit hungry, but I feel like I've been asleep for a week and I need to go for a run."

"Three weeks," he said.

"I'm sorry?"

"You were asleep for three weeks."

"Three weeks?"

Henry smiled as if it were a great joke, and stepped off the verandah. Morag and the dog trailing behind him.

"Yes, we had to get Dr Corrington out to look at you."

"Ffffu... I'm so sorry to put you to all that trouble."

She caught up to him, and he tucked her arm through his.

"Nonsense, you've given us all something to talk about."

They took the short route around the Central Lawn and up to the lake.

"So, how did you manage to get inside the house without anyone seeing you?" he asked.

"I told you. I live in the Hall, and I just opened the door. It's the first time I've seen it as your bedroom."

"But if you live in the house in the future, how is this the first time you've seen my bedroom."

Morag paused in the middle of the bridge across the lake, looking out over the water. Dante sat with a small thump.

"I guess seeing as I've fixed it, there's no harm in telling you about it.

"There was some kind of incident on the 9th of September, 1904 that somehow uncoupled you and your room from the rest of the house. So, whenever I opened the door, I never knew when or where you would be."

Henry leaned his back against the railings, looking in the other direction, "it sounds incredible. But you said you had proof?"

"I do, but your fiancé took my locket."

Henry stiffened, and Morag hastily backtracked, "I'm sure she's just keeping it safe for me until I leave."

Henry sagged so much Morag turned to support him.

"Well, I believe that solves one of my problems."

"Is there something wrong?"

He smiled, "No Morag, there's nothing for *you* to be concerned about."

Henry set a fast pace back across the bridge, taking the even shorter cut through the pavilion, skirting the pool, and back through the main entrance.

A man met them there, "ah Barnes," Henry said, "would you please ask Mrs Lewis to make up some morning tea and have it brought to the Drawing Room?"

"Yes Sir."

"And do you know where my mother and Miss Seagrove are?"

"I believe your mother is in the Drawing Room Sir, but I'm not sure where Miss Seagrove is."

"Good, make it three for morning tea then. I'll be back with you momentarily."

Mrs Fox was seated on a small sofa embroidering something. She was a small woman, dressed in a relatively simple black dress with a white lace collar and cuffs. She looked up as they entered.

Dante ran to her and sat, leaning on her leg as he slumped to the ground panting.

"Wait here," he said to Morag, then sat next to his mother to hold a whispered conversation. Now and again, she nodded.

Morag feigned an interest in the artwork and vases of flowers.

A young woman arrived with a big tray of sandwiches and cake, followed by an older woman with a large pot of tea, and another with plates, cutlery, cups and saucers.

They deposited them on the now empty coffee table.

Henry beckoned her over, "Mother, may I present Miss Clementine, Miss Clementine, my mother Mrs Fox."

Unsure of the protocol, she sketched a curtsy just in case

Mrs Fox snorted an unladylike snort, "there's no need for that."

She patted the seat beside her, "Henry tells me you haven't had any breakfast, why don't you sit here next to me and eat something."

As Henry left the room, Morag didn't have to be asked twice.

Henry smiled grimly; Barnes was still waiting just outside the Drawing Room.

"Come with me," he said, heading towards the stairwell.

On the first floor, he headed to the small dressing room which had been converted to a bedroom to accommodate Miss Seagrove.

He knocked on the door, and there was no answer, so he opened it.

The room was a shambles. He was so sure the prim Miss Seagrove wouldn't condone this kind of mess, he was half convinced there'd been another burglary.

Until he noticed his mother's ivory fan on the dressing table. And his favourite lapis lazuli cuff links. Along with some other trinkets his brothers and sisters had "lost" since the blasted woman had arrived.

For a moment he considered the embarrassment Mr and Mrs Seagrove would face when he sent her back.

But then he thought about how rude she was to the servants and his siblings. Not to mention the things she'd said about Miss Clementine without giving her the chance to defend herself.

And to top it off, that she had dared to threaten them with the things she would do once she was married to him.

It could not be condoned.

"Barnes do you see our missing items there on the dresser?"

"Yes Sir."

"Would you collect it all, and arrange someone to pack Miss Seagrove's belongings."

"Yes Sir."

"Only the things we can be sure she brought with her. Miss Clementine complained Miss Seagrove took her locket, so mind we don't pack anything she hasn't been seen in before."

Barnes nodded and collected the jewellery together. Henry closed the door behind them.

He watched Barnes head towards the staff quarters, then went into the Master Suite where he paced up and down swearing violently, thinking he needed something like a gymnasium to take his feelings out of him.

Instead, he threw his jacket on a chair, went to his bathroom, and splashed cold water on his face.

He sighed and thought some more about Morag.

The hungry way she'd looked at him when she thought he wasn't watching, and the support she'd offered him without knowing he was shocked by Miss Seagrove's misrepresentation of their relationship.

He barely knew Morag, but he liked her. She was easy to be around, not demanding like Miss Seagrove.

He thought she was the kind of person who'd want to read the newspaper in the morning, and imagined bickering amiably with her about that at the breakfast table.

And he remembered their brisk walk about the gardens, how he'd struggled to make her walk at a lady-like pace.

Given the chance, Morag would challenge him and his assumptions every day of his life, but he would enjoy it.

Smiling a little at the thought, he turned to collect his jacket and found Miss Seagrove with a kitchen knife.

Which was a little funny as he hadn't thought she might even know where the kitchen was.

She advanced into the bathroom, holding it out in front of her, "I won't let her have you," she said, "you belong to me."

Henry held his hands up towards her, "think about what you're saying, Miss Seagrove."

Her face contorted, and she put on a whiny voice to say, "Miss Seagrove, Miss Seagrove." She slashed the knife downwards as she made a noise of frustration, bringing it up again as she asked, "why in God's name won't you call me Viola?"

There wasn't really anything to say to that, so he shrugged, an act that enraged her.

She screamed and lunged towards him, he backed away into the space between the sink and bath, blocking her slash with his forearm and slipping to the ground.

And then screamed again as Miss Clementine slammed her arm into the rim of the bathtub forcing her to drop the knife, and then up behind her back before she could defend herself.

"You right there mate?" she asked as if nothing untoward had happened.

Miss Seagrove was squirming to get away, but Barnes and Roberts had arrived on the scene and carried the kicking and screaming girl away.

"Hey," she called, and the men paused, "send someone back with some bandages okay?" Roberts nodded.

Miss Clementine...

Morag squatted down to his level, "you sure? You look a bit peaky."

She offered him a hand up, but he pulled her down and into a kiss.

Which she returned with the kind of intensity that suggested long term practice.

He was insanely jealous of his future self.

After a time, she pulled away, "you should let me treat that arm."

Reluctantly he held his hand up, and she had no difficulty pulling him up.

Despite himself, he was impressed.

She grabbed a towel, and helped him across to the seat, throwing the towel into his lap as she removed his tie and started unbuttoning his shirt.

He trapped her hand in his, "I'm not sure this is appropriate."

"Don't be ridiculous, you'll bleed to death at this rate. And if you don't, penicillin hasn't been invented yet so you'll die of blood poisoning later."

"Penny what?" he said and dropped his hand, and let her continue.

"Hmmm, not too serious though it looks like you might need stitches. I'll bind it tightly until the doctor can get here." She folded the towel and pressed it against his wound, "hold this tight."

He heard her rummaging around in the bathroom before reappearing with his cologne, "ok, I'm going to pour this on your wound, and it's going to hurt about a billion more times than hell. Okay?"

Almost before she'd finished speaking, she'd started pouring, and it did indeed hurt a billion times more than hell, but he clenched his teeth together and bore it.

Roberts arrived with bandages, "wait," she said to him.

"Ready for more?" she asked Henry folding one of the bandages quickly.

He nodded uncertainly.

She placed the folded bandage on the wound, directed Roberts to hold it, and the arm tightly, then started winding the bandage around his arm to hold it in place. She used her teeth to tear the bandage and tie it around his wrist.

"A couple of pillows please," she said to Roberts and held his arm up above his head until he brought them back. She laid the pillows in his lap and rested his elbow on them, "keep your arm up Henry, it will help stop the bleeding."

"Your blouse," he said looking at the blood.

She grinned, "I don't have to do the laundry while I'm here right?"

Mrs Fox entered the room, "good God," she said when she saw the state of them both. "Did Miss Seagrove cause this?"

Morag made a dismissive noise, "it's nothing."

"We've telephoned for Dr Corrington; he shouldn't be too long He's got a new car and has been itching to try it out.

"Miss Clementine—"

"I think you might call me Morag after this," she waved her hand at Henry.

Mrs Fox inclined her head, "then perhaps you could call me Lily."

"Thank you Lily."

"Morag, perhaps you might like to change your clothes?"

She looked down her body, "I can see that might be the wisest use of my time right now."

She turned to walk away.

"Wait," Henry cried, "what did you come to see me for?"

"What?

"Oh right. Mrs... Lily sent me to see if you were joining us downstairs."

"I expect I might be delayed."

Morag laughed as she left the room.

《《 • 》》

Of all the things she had seen and done in the last five years with Henry, this had to have been the most exciting. Awake for a day, and she'd saved his life a second time.

Amazing.

And Lily seemed to like her too.

She shimmied out of the blood-stained blue skirt and white blouse, and replaced it with a robe she found in the wardrobe. She went to the bathroom to wash her face, chest and hands.

Back in her room, she donned a russet brown skirt, and a cream, pin-tucked blouse. Then, figuring she should at least put the clothes in to soak, she walked down the back stairs and through to the laundry room.

Of course, it was not the same as her modern house, and she had no idea what to do with all the buckets, mangles, and other equipment she didn't have the names for.

Happily, the young woman with the sandwich tray was on hand to help.

And having been reminded of the sandwiches, she returned to the Drawing Room, and happily for her, the food was still there.

So she helped herself to another sandwich.

And thought about present Henry.

Who wasn't engaged to Miss Seagrove.

And who seemed to like her.

A lot.

He wasn't her Henry, and she felt conflicted about that, but she was quite confident she was stuck in 1904.

With this Henry.

And a Henry in the hand was worth two in the bush.

Dante sat next to her, and she absently fed him a sandwich.

If she couldn't go back to her time, then she would rather be here with a Henry, than out there alone.

If he would have her.

She sat on a sofa in the bay window, looking out into the roses.

And yawned.

Then undid her shoelaces, toed her boots off, and lay down on the sofa. With a scrabble of claws, Dante got up on the couch and snuggled between her legs and the back of the sofa.

《《 • 》》

Henry found them together when he brought Dr Corrington into the Drawing Room to check her over.

Dr Corrington chuckled, and Dante rested his chin on her knees.

"Looks like she's scored another fan," he said scratching Dante's head. "Let's leave her be. By all accounts, she's had an eventful day and probably needs her sleep."

His mother saw the doctor out, while he dropped into a seat and helped himself to a sandwich.

"She's certainly a remarkable woman," he said to his mother as she entered the room.

Mrs Fox sat beside him and stretched her feet out, "if what Dr Corrington said is true, she saved your life."

He pulled the locket he thought was Morag's out of his pocket, and started sliding the pieces around.

"But for what?" he answered, and then told her what Morag'd said about his future.

She thought for a moment, then suggested, "I know she thinks she's averted that future, but you would be wise to look into how you can protect your interests for the future. Open a trust or something."

He didn't want to think about that, but future Henry seemed wise enough to have done something like that.

All of a sudden, the locket fell to pieces in his lap, leaving him holding some small pictures.

He and his mother put their heads together to look at them. The woman was definitely Morag, and the man certainly looked like Henry.

"Shanghai 2216," came a voice behind them, making them jump.

Henry looked up at her, and shuffled to the next picture, "Paris 1925," at the next, "New York 2036," and the next, "The *Destiny* 2765."

Henry flicked through the pictures, looking for something to tell him she was lying.

It still seemed preposterous.

He stood up, dropping the pieces on the floor, "I don't really care where you came from. I just want you to stay. Will you stay?"

Morag snorted, "It's not like men are beating down the door wanting to marry me, and I don't actually have anywhere else to go. Of course I'll stay!"

His mother averted her eyes and helped herself to cake while he kissed Morag within an inch of her life.

THE END

THE MYSTERY OF
THE MASTER SUITE

If there is one thing that almost everyone who has ever been married knows, it's that the lead up to the day is terrifying and exhilarating by turns.

While there is a special thrill to be had by attending Church to hear the banns being read, and the congregation praying for you, it doesn't really do much for your peace of mind.

Except perhaps for that five minutes when everyone's calming thoughts are focused on you.

But the minute you leave the building, it's back to worrying about the arrangements.

And in this respect, Miss Morag Clementine, late of twenty-first-century Melbourne worried about them a lot less than her fiancé Mr Henry Fox, and her mother-in-law to be, who were much more invested in the proprieties.

After all, it was the year 1905, and they had reputations to maintain.

In the nine months since Morag'd arrived with no warning, and no logical explanation, her short, dark, red hair had grown into the kind of bob that wouldn't become fashionable for another ten years or so.

She'd relaxed into floor-length skirts, and the hair on her legs was almost as luxuriant as that on her head.

Morag summarily rejected the tightly corseted S-curve silhouette of the Gibson Girl and embraced the two-piece walking ensemble of trumpet skirt and blouse.

She was particularly fond of a tightly tailored jacket, and thankfully our dressmaker was exceptional at tailoring.

This was the outfit she could be seen *running* around the gardens in, often accompanied by Dante the pug, and sometimes by fiancé Henry Fox who had trouble keeping up with her.

Our Henry, it has to be said, being a man of his time, was rather too fond of rich food and too much wine.

She first met her groom in 2020, coincidentally in the same house as she was living in 1905. She hadn't realised how fond she was of future Henry until she'd left him.

At his insistence.

By going back to the day he'd got lost in time to prevent him from triggering the event.

Through which method she'd lost that Henry by becoming stuck in time herself.

With our present-day...

Or maybe her past Henry.

Or, seeing as she was marrying him, maybe even her future Henry.

Time paradoxes can be quite hard to get your head around.

There was no doubt in her mind, that the 1905 version of Henry was the better looking of the two, mainly because he didn't carry the cares of a century with him.

But also, because his perfectly ordinary brown hair and eyes seemed much brighter by contrast with his lush reddish-brown moustache.

Though without the exposure to other ideas and cultures, he could be a little, well, backwards. Or to put it more charitably, traditional.

Being possibly the most modern of modern women at that time, she'd moved into the Master suite almost before he'd asked her to stay with him. And made him bring her in a tiny desk she'd found in the attic so she could sit at it in the big bay window.

I'm not sure she truly believed she had "fixed" him; that he was fully anchored in time with her instead of travelling to a different time and place every day.

I think she wanted to be there to make sure our Henry stayed in 1905 with her. Or at the very least, that he couldn't leave without her.

Though to be honest, it sounds to me that travelling to a different place every day might be better than staying in the stifling atmosphere of Hayward Hall.

Morag would've been perfectly happy without a wedding, but scandalised, our family wasn't having any of that.

Like I say, she was very modern. I for one found her refusal to accept any limitations inspiring.

So, the wedding was on, but they couldn't persuade her to observe the proprieties and move back out of his rooms.

The last of the banns had been read, and she was facing her last week of singledom.

Bearing in mind how... let's say tense, she became when he tried to discuss any of the more feminine arts with her, he'd screwed up his courage and suggested she might like to redecorate the house.

Morag assured him the heavy mahogany furniture would be worth a fortune one day, (presumably, she knew that for a fact). Not to mention that she adored its "retro effect" (whatever that was) and that the suite was large enough to render said furniture small by comparison.

However, given the opportunity, she would adore a nice blue Chinoiserie wallpaper.

Okay, that's not exactly what she said, but half the time we didn't know what she was talking about.

Except when it came to the coffee.

The late nineteenth-century coffee craze had largely passed us by, but Morag was barely civil without several cups of it in the morning.

She liked it in a big cup of warm milk, which we found fascinating, and which was unbelievably delicious.

As the day of the wedding grew closer and closer, Morag started taking longer and longer runs to calm her nerves.

And spending more and more time in the library, busily reading books and newspapers to catch up on current events, fashion and etiquette.

Morag particularly liked looking at the spreads in the society pages about Henry and her.

She'd lean on her arm, and look at the photographs and say, "imagine that, some chick from

Footscray marrying the most eligible bachelor of the decade."

She practised her gossiping on us and it was hilarious. She hadn't come from a large family like ours, and we could tell she was trying to fit in with us, and with 1905.

One time I heard her crying with the stress of it.

The day of Wednesday, August 30, 1905, dawned bitterly cold, squally and showery. In some small towns 20 miles or so out of the city, snowfalls as much as two feet had been recorded.

The wedding was of course at the old St Clements in Elsternwick, not the new brick one, but the wooden one that was there before it. With the Reverend George Sproule presiding. It was a very modest affair, with only close friends and family in attendance.

You could give or take Henry in his morning suit, but Morag was radiant and beautiful.

She'd designed her own gown, cream, with a lace V neck cross-over bodice and a heavy satin notched skirt, though she said she copied someone called Jeanne Paquin.

A reception was to be held at the house, and Mama had made a special effort to decorate the ballroom with garlands of white roses from the garden.

Not herself obviously, but she directed it.

The original plan was to pose for some photographs in the garden, but that was out of the question with the weather.

Mr Smythe, the head gardener, who shared Morag's interest in orchids, had decorated the conservatory with orchids and ferns.

It made a splendid backdrop for the photographs.

They did make a beautiful couple, even in the massive family shots.

And the slightly awkward shots with the servants.

You could tell they were deeply in love.

When the prints came out, they were spectacular.

Morag excused herself to freshen up before the dinner.

Henry kissed her neck because she'd already started walking towards the stairs, "hurry back," he called after her.

She turned and smiled, and in her characteristic style, she said, "oh, I will."

The photographer took some more pictures of the family, and the conservatory, and the rainy weather, and after a while, our Henry started looking at his watch.

And it wasn't too long before he said, "Amelia, go check on her," and because I was curious, I did.

Instead of back-chatting him.

I suppose I should mention that at this point, I was just his fifteen-year-old sister. Third youngest in the family, and usually confined to the nursery with the twins.

Dante, who by this point was more Morag's dog than Mama's, came haring after me.

I did a quick swoop through the ground floor rooms, though I didn't call her name as the guests were already assembling and I didn't want to alarm them.

Then I ran upstairs and I heard her screaming.

Not a short, sharp scream like a girl might make when you sneak up on her.

Or the kind of long, drawn-out scream you might make when you're attacked by something.

But the sort of grunting sound Morag makes when she's practising her unarmed combat.

Plus, I could hear the sounds of a scuffle, so I ran towards the Master suite, calling her name.

Dante, barking furiously, beat me to the closed door.

I heard her say, "No! Wait. I need..."

And when we burst in the door a few seconds later there was no one there.

Not Morag, and not the person she was asking to wait.

Her chair had been knocked over, the top of her desk was empty, and papers were spread all around the desk as if she'd been grasping at it for something to hold on to.

The beautiful, engraved silver fountain pen Henry gave her as an engagement gift was on the other side of the room.

As if she'd thrown it at her attacker to deflect them.

The net curtains waved wildly in the stiff breeze through the window.

Though seeing as she always had the windows open, no matter the weather, I ignored them.

Dante ran around the room, barking his way through the dressing room and onto the bathroom, and I followed him calling her name.

She didn't answer, and there was no sign of her.

On our way back, I opened the bathroom and dressing room doors but didn't see anyone, or anything suspicious in either corridor.

Dante spent a lot of time sniffing around her desk and trotting from window to window whining.

With nothing else to go on, I looked out of the windows.

The ground floor had a roofed verandah underneath so, it would have been possible to climb out the window, crawl across the roof, then shimmy down a column to the ground.

At least it was possible to do all that from the nursery window so I saw no reason to doubt it was possible from the master.

But I didn't see how you could make Morag do that without a fight.

And a great deal of noise.

Unless she was unconscious.

I couldn't see anything on the ground from my vantage point.

A shiver ran down my spine, not just from the cold wind.

There was nothing for it, but to tell Henry his bride was missing.

Dante refused to leave the room. He lay down under the desk, back to the room, resting his nose on his paws.

Henry didn't take the news well.

"That's not possible," he said, "I don't believe it."

And ran through the house, ignoring well-wishers, and up the stairs. Ignoring Dante, he conducted his own search of the suite.

I waited on his bed.

He slumped down beside me, running his fingers through his hair.

"She can't be gone," he said, looking hopefully at me.

I didn't know what to do, so I shrugged.

Henry started crying like a girl.

Shortly after that Roberts, Henry's valet arrived.

"Henry, what's wrong?"

Henry blubbered something, and Roberts looked at me to translate.

"Morag's gone missing. I heard her call out just before I came in."

He looked around the room, and at Henry, mostly useless on the bed.

Roberts clearly had no idea what to do either.

"Right," I said, "you find Barnes, tell him what's happened, and ask him to telephone the police. I'll find Nanny and see if she has a syrup or something that might help Henry."

Roberts tugged his vest down, squared his shoulders and nodded.

We went our separate ways.

By the time I had found Nanny, convinced her to leave the twins on their best behaviour, helped her find the laudanum, and got back to Henry, he was asleep, curled up on the bed with Dante.

I left Nanny with him, then went back downstairs to tell the rest of the family.

About the time they'd got over, "I don't believe it," and "It's impossible," Barnes announced, "the Police are on their way."

Mama managed to get a grip on herself, saying "let's go into the Drawing Room to wait."

And asking Barnes, "would you please fetch us all a tot of whisky for the shock?"

Barnes came to me last and looked at me for what seemed like a very long time before he gave me a tiny slosh in a glass.

I was already thinking five steps ahead of everyone else, and I asked him, "have you been checking the guests off the list as they arrived?"

He looked at me a bit more, frowning.

Or maybe thinking.

They don't call me Trouble for nothing.

"No. We've been rushing the guests through into the ballroom, and directing the cars onto the gravel."

"So, there's no real way to be sure who's here and who isn't? Or whether we have any wedding crashers?"

"Our servants would recognise many of the guests, but I suppose it can't be ruled out."

The photographer had been hired to take pictures of the family, not the reception. But he was still hanging around in the conservatory, not quite sure what to do with himself given the news.

Barnes looked at me like he knew what I was thinking.

I threw the drink back like I'd seen Morag do, and eyes watering, managed to breathe out the fumes without squeaking.

"Quite," said Barnes

A moment later, I felt nicely relaxed, but as if my brain was working overtime.

The way I saw it, we had about 260 suspects in the house; the wedding guests and the five footmen hired to help out at the wedding.

I went back to the photographer and told him Mama had asked him to take photos of the guests. I escorted him to the ballroom; he couldn't seem to believe his luck and set up the camera and started taking pictures.

Now that I'd taken care of identifying the guests as far as possible, there were two others with histories that I knew of.

Miss Viola Seagrove who had been sent from the house in disgrace after she'd attacked Henry with a kitchen knife.

And Mr Edward Curry, Henry's former best friend, who'd decided Morag was a gold digger and set out to prove it.

I couldn't do anything about those two, except make sure the police were aware of them when they arrived.

Being only fifteen, I had read too many detective novels and had formed the opinion that all detectives were either geniuses like Sherlock Holmes or less than intellectually gifted like Inspector Lestrade.

And sadly, Inspector Morrison of St Kilda station, a portly man with a very tall top hat, turned out to be the latter.

In those days, children were supposed to be seen and not heard, though more often than not, it was that people chose not to see or hear them. Though of course the twins and I would hang around collecting other people's secrets.

Anyway, Inspector Morrison considered a fifteen-year-old girl, with her nose stuck in a book to be of such little note that he very didn't bother to chase me away from the library where he conducted the interviews.

And I eavesdropped shamelessly.

I'm not altogether convinced Morag would have approved, but it seemed the only way I could get to the bottom of the situation was to conduct my own investigation.

The first of Inspector Morrison's shortcomings was his starting assumption that Morag had "probably been overcome with emotion and run away."

Mama and my siblings were outraged at the suggestion, talking at cross purposes over each other.

Why for heaven's sake we wondered?

Why would she do it *after* the ceremony when clearly Morag would have just said no if she didn't want to get married.

Especially in that weather.

Admittedly I wasn't a hardboiled detective by any means, but I just couldn't see what was to be gained by a woman lighting out of a place within an hour of her wedding.

It wasn't until Barnes brought her coat into the Drawing Room that Inspector Morrison was persuaded she hadn't voluntarily left the house.

The Inspector's second shortcoming was that he saw no need to comb the gardens for clues.

Admittedly he had brought only one other officer with him, and it was raining cats and dogs, but it seemed he still wanted to believe Morag had left of her own volition.

Poor kidnapped Morag could have been knocked out and secreted in one of the dozens of sheds, glass-houses and other storage places across 30 acres of ground.

When I made the suggestion, Mr Smythe was only too happy to send gardeners out walking the paths and checking the structures for any signs of Morag.

To be honest, I didn't have much hope, the weather would wash out all but the most determined steps. But my main concern was to be sure she wasn't being held on the property.

And if she was, to bring her back into the house as soon as possible.

Not to mention that there might be some other kind of suspicious behaviour.

Miss Seagrove or Mr Curry might have found their way onto the property, but not been seen by anyone at the house.

The way the Inspector Morrison saw it, there were twenty suspects; the servants.

And if the servants didn't turn out to have done it, then perhaps the aforementioned Seagrove or Curry.

Or both of them together.

Morag would've been furious that they would dare to suspect our servant's loyalty, but I suppose they weren't keen to start interviewing the "quality" about their whereabouts.

Inspector Morrison's third shortcoming was to disregard the family, both their beliefs and their knowledge.

As soon as I realised he was going to let the guests go home, I sent the twins lurking in the Ballroom to see who was there, and what they were talking about, and whether anyone said or did anything suspicious.

Fortunately, Mama also sent the older four children to help clear everyone out of the ballroom.

In the meantime, I made myself comfortable in the library while Inspector Morrison started interviewing the staff.

It was clear he rented a full board room in a boarding house; he had no idea how busy a house this size keeps the servants.

Or the amount of time and effort it takes to prepare for a wedding.

Barnes and Mrs Rose the housekeeper were busy supervising the maids and temporary footmen. Even Nanny was pitching in or at least making sure the twins didn't wreck the place.

Or both at the same time.

"Yes, Inspector," Barnes reassured him, "they had *all* been setting up the glasses for champagne and laying out snacks".

Roberts and Prince, Morag's lady's maid, had been together, packing the trunks for the honeymoon.

Dodds the chauffeur had put the car away; no luggage, meant nothing further to do until it was ready to be loaded.

In the meantime, he helped the gardeners lugging the pot plants around in the conservatory for the photographs, and then clearing away the debris.

Once the luggage was ready, one of the gardeners helped him load it up, and in the usual course of events would have helped him unload when they got to Spencer Street Station.

With all the servants alibied out, Inspector Morrison asked whether anyone might have slipped away.

Our servants were too polite to roll their eyes the way I did.

Of course, it was possible. Anyone could have slipped away.

Anyone who didn't want a job anymore at any rate.

Anyone who didn't care about the rest of the household being so busy.

And when you have such a small household, you're generally quite close with the other servants and the family.

I couldn't help wondering why he didn't factor the family into his calculations.

Of course, we were all in the conservatory for the photographs, but he didn't know that.

And just as the servants could slip away, so could the family.

Stephen certainly did, though he only went as far as the Drawing Room for a glass of wine.

Though Mama did frown at him.

As the Inspector took his leave, Mama asked him to look into the whereabouts of Miss Seagrove and Mr Curry.

I wasn't sure he would comply; he was still giving me the vibe of Morag leaving of her own volition.

Mr Smythe came back with the news that there was no sign of Morag in any of the outbuildings and no sign of any suspicious activity.

Barnes discretely handed me the invitation list, in which was recorded the invitees and their RSVPs.

The photographer took his leave, saying the photographs would be available in a week.

We sat in the Drawing Room for a while, but no one said anything. One of the maids brought us tea and some sandwiches.

I was starving, and the twins too.

We ate the sandwiches, but no one else seemed to have much of an appetite.

I suppose it was a big day for them.

Mama went for a lie-down, and my brothers and sisters went their own ways.

I went to check on Henry, and neither he nor Dante seemed to have moved. They were both snoring gently, and Nanny was nowhere to be seen.

Perhaps she'd gone downstairs to the kitchen to be with the other staff.

The twins and I reconvened in the nursery, which had recently been converted into a schoolroom, with had lots of blackboard space.

Space for my lessons, space for Rosanna's lessons, and space for Roland's lessons.

I assumed the Inspector would follow up with interviews of Seagrove and Curry.

I expected he would carry them out away at the police station, and that he would let us know.

Or I suppose more correctly, Henry or Mama.

With the guest list, we had some evidence of who was in the house. We were discussing the people they'd seen when Stephen wandered in to see what we were doing.

It was too late to cover the boards, and I couldn't come up with a reasonable excuse so I told him the truth.

We were trying to work out who had the opportunity to capture Morag.

"Hold on a minute," he said and left the room, reappearing a short while later with all the other children except Henry.

With nine of us together, we started from the beginning - what I had seen and heard.

I didn't have a watch, but through a series of dramatic re-enactments, we concluded you'd need at least four kidnappers to abduct Morag.

Two in the room to subdue her and get her out of the window, two on the ground to catch her and hide in the bushes until I'd left the room.

We estimated perhaps five minutes to accomplish that, and given the Ballroom was on the opposite side of the building, it would be possible to do that out of sight of the guests.

The question was, had I given them enough time to conceal themselves, and I had to admit that the few minutes Dante and I had spent running around the room would have been enough to conceal themselves.

We expected that two people could have abducted her, but it would have taken longer.

It was possible a guest, or guests, had been involved in the kidnapping, but no one noticed any guests who were wetter than the circumstances warranted.

I started to feel quite sad because it was beginning to look as though someone, perhaps Miss Seagrove or Mr Curry, had commissioned the kidnapping.

Nonetheless, we started sorting out the guest list, checking off the expected guests who had been seen, or referred to by other guests.

We were left with a few guests who we couldn't verify.

I decided to check with Barnes to see if he had seen them, and shortly after that, we were able to check them off the list too.

We were left with the option of two or four unknown people, disabling her, and kidnapping her out of her own bedroom.

It was unsupportable.

The next day Inspector Morrison called back at the house to notify us that Miss Seagrove was with her parents at Lakes Entrance, and had been for several months. And Mr Curry had taken the train to Sydney at the beginning of the year.

Neither of them could have known about the wedding.

We were left with no rational explanation for her disappearance.

By lunchtime, Roberts and I bullied Henry out of his bed, and into the bathroom to bathe.

With the door open, Dante ran downstairs, presumably concerned for his own ablutions.

While they were occupied, I picked up Morag's papers from the floor, and I noticed a dark stain on the floor under the desk, I knelt down to see if Dante had left a mess, but it smelled like a burn.

How had it got there?

When I picked up the fountain pen, I notice another, smaller char mark on the carpet, and in some places, the engraving had a kind of drip pattern that I was fairly sure hadn't been there before.

I straightened the papers up on her desk, and naturally, I looked at them.

Her handwriting was atrocious.

There was a list of dates, starting with September 9, 1904, the date she arrived, and followed by August 30, 1905, today's date.

Then a sequence of dates leading up to March 15, 2211. And a separate series of dates ending February 21, 2194. What were the dates about?

There were pages of notes about weather conditions going back several months; freak tornadoes, unexpected snowstorms, and lightning strikes.

Was she perhaps not looking at the news as much as the weather?

And finally, there was a hurried note to Henry, one that broke off mid-sentence.

> *I don't think we got it right. I don't think it was the watch.*
>
> *I think it was an astrological conjunction combined with an unusual weather pattern.*
>
> *If something happens to me, don't try to find me.*
>
> *I'm happy knowing I saved you. I hope you...*

As I said, there was no rational explanation for her disappearance, but was it possible that the same freak conditions that had brought her here, had taken her away again?

It wasn't exactly plausible, but it wasn't exactly implausible either.

And with no rational explanation for Morag's disappearance, we had no option but to believe the unbelievable.

THE END

THE GHOST DETECTORS

Zoo yawned and sighed to loosen his jaw as he looked through the spear tipped wrought iron gates, up at the house beyond.

He felt the kind of frisson that suggested the shoot was going to be a good one.

He turned and walked past the gates to the edge of the property, continuing his vocal warm up exercises by humming up and down a couple of octaves.

When the property had been built, it was situated in close to 30 hectares of gardens.

But since the tragic events of 1905, it had been sold off little, by little, until all that remained was a monstrous house in an inappropriately small garden.

One of the gates hung drunkenly from a crumbling brick pillar, and he wondered how he could incorporate that into the show.

He pulled a stainless-steel straw from his pocket, put it in his mouth, and hummed up and down his vocal range.

As he looked up at the two-story house, he pulled a bottle of water from his bullet harness inspired tool belt and hummed a few bars of his favourite song down the straw and into the water.

Set the drone to rush down through the gates, over the overgrown drive and up to the wreckage of the portico?

He dropped the straw into the bottle and buzzed his lips, making them vibrate.

Nah, too hackneyed.

He walked back to the other side of the property, rolling his tongue, saying rrrrr up and down his range, trying a very little to expand it.

From the outside, it looked exactly like what you'd expect of a haunted house.

The land sales had resulted in the front door facing a street that was no longer there.

The side door, once with views over the croquet lawn, had become the de facto front door.

Consequently, the house had the appearance of turning away from you, though Zoo couldn't tell whether it was ashamed of what it had become, or whether it thought he was beneath its notice.

He was a man for whom all things are either black or white - no shades of grey. He liked straight lines and order; each of his avenues of interest were neatly compartmentalised away from all the others.

It was what made him so good at hosting *The Ghost Detectors* show.

Despite being the kind of person who would go into a stranger's home and straighten the pictures.

Though the fans loved it - home owners freaking out on camera, and he would coolly adjust the hang of a picture. It was almost his signature move.

Though of course, he didn't believe any of it. All mass hysteria.

The "new" drive up to the house bisected the lawn, enough off centre to make him uncomfortable

The garden, if you could call it that, was overgrown. Full-height trees and bushes had taken over the lawn so comprehensively that it would only be possible to mow the grass on your hands and knees, blade by blade.

He flexed his jaw, yawning with his mouth closed.

The fountain on his left had once featured a woman in ancient draperies pouring water from an urn on her shoulder, but a lightning strike had split the statue in half and melted the fountain mechanism.

Or so the story went.

He pulled back to the side of the street, singing eeeee as he worked his way up two octaves, and ohhhhh as he sang down again. Once more trying a very little to increase his range.

The walls of the house remained at two stories, with a tower reaching a third on his right. The roof had caved in across several rooms, probably about the same time the portico collapsed.

Zoo stood, hands on hips, singing ooooo like a demented siren as he looked through the gate.

The yellow bricks were still clearly visible against the red, the diamond patterns still discernible through the dirt.

For a moment he thought he saw a woman silhouetted in a second story window, then realised it was sun glare.

Zoo sang his scales again, and only then permitted himself to drink some water.

Then he checked his tool harness for the necessities; torch, walkie talkie, notebook and pen, his phone, a Polaroid camera, voice recorder, his electromagnetic field detector, thermal camera, the Kinect camera, spirit box, ghost box, and motion detector.

Even though Brian, tech and comedic relief guy, had already checked them.

Pulling each device out of the harness, turning it on, checking the power, and putting it back again.

Camera operator Steve was taking background shots of the gates, house, and garden, while Josh set up the fixed camera feed to the laptop.

They had both daylight and night vision, focused on the house exterior. The cameras would record the team entering and exiting the building, along with any other phenomenon.

Brian was checking the portable cameras Steve and Josh would be using to film inside the house.

"Ready?" Zoo asked the team.

The men replied in the affirmative.

They walked across to where the midnight blue sports utility vehicle branded with *The Ghost Detectors* decal was backed up just inside the gates.

Steve started filming the introduction that would play before the title sequence, and while they walked across the lawn.

Zoo talked through the history as he spread the floor plans out on the bonnet.

"Mr Dewitt Fox, made his fortune selling goods in the Victorian Goldfields, and built Hayward Hall in 1868 with the proceeds.

"This house has seen many deaths, starting with Dewitt and ending with the suicide of Lucy Chalmers just five years ago.

"It's also seen the mysterious disappearances of two women named Morag Clementine, one in 1905, and one in 2030, and Henry Fox in 1922.

"The most haunted rooms are reputed to be the library," he pulled the ground floor plan to the top and pointed out the library.

"And the master bedroom," he pulled the ground floor plan aside to reveal the second story, and indicated that room.

"Reported phenomenon include hearing footsteps running up and down the stairs located here," he tapped the stairs on both floor plans, doors opening and closing themselves, objects falling from shelves, and of course, temperature changes."

Zoo looked around the group, "any questions?"

Brian asked, "How do you open the door to a haunted house?"

Josh rolled his eyes and replied, "with a skeleton key."

The all groaned while Zoo folded the floor plans and tucked them in his tool belt.

Steve waited a moment, and then said, "clear."

They regrouped just inside the focus of the fixed cameras, and Josh turned them on.

Zoo stood in the middle as the "star" of the show.

They waited for a moment, then Zoo called the crew together, "all right then, let's get this show on the road."

He rubbed his hands together, holding one each out to Steve and Josh as they walked into frame. Brian joined hands with Steve and Josh on the other side, careful to keep Zoo framed in the centre.

Zoo prayed out loud, "gods and goddesses of life, please protect us as we venture into the realm of the dead, and bring us safely out again.

"Gods and goddesses of the dead, let us pass through your realm safely and unharmed. And if your subjects are here in this place, please let us speak with them and hear their stories, and when we leave, keep only those who are yours.

"So be it."

And the men echoed him, "so be it."

"All right then," Zoo said to camera as the team backed up to fan around him, "it's sunset and we're here at Hayward Hall, possibly the most haunted house in Melbourne. As always, we go in live, and you get to come with us."

They turned their backs to the camera, and Zoo looked back over his shoulder, "are you ready?

"Then let's go!"

They walked, or perhaps more correctly waded across the garden towards the house.

As they got close, Steve and Josh pulled out the cameras and started filming.

Zoo and Brian waited until filming had started, then turned their tool belt equipment on, took their EMF detectors out and pointed them here and there as if trying to get a mobile phone signal.

"All fine so far," Zoo said, and Brian nodded.

Zoo climbed over a pile of rubble and up to the door, taking the key from his pocket and opening the door. It opened smoothly, and they walked inside.

"If you're wondering why the house is fairly well maintained," he told Steve and the audience, "Henry Fox set up a trust in 1908 to maintain the house. It remained intact until 2025 when Lucy Chalmers became the trustee, dissolved the trust, and used the funds to pay for her lavish lifestyle."

They walked through the door, across a small alcove and into a larger room.

"This area was originally the drawing room, and the library is just across the corridor."

The camera men panned across the room, highlighting the dust and peeling wallpaper, the sheet music still resting on the piano, the spotted mirror above the fireplace.

It was hard to know whether the ceiling had originally been painted, or whether the mould growth had made its own design.

Brian suppressed a scream, and Josh filmed his face. He shrugged, "I thought I saw someone," he said.

Zoo held his EMF detector up to show Steve he had two bars lit up. He tucked it back in his belt, pulled out the Polaroid, and took a picture in Brian's direction.

"With all this stuff still in here, it's hard to know whether you're looking at something paranormal or not."

Brian rubbed his temples, "this place is giving me a headache."

"Let's go across to the library," Zoo said, and Brian nodded.

Part of the library's ceiling had fallen down, leaving the beams exposed, and dislodging some of the books as it fell.

A long red hued wood table was stacked with books, almost as if someone had popped out of the room for just a moment, and would be back any minute.

Steve panned across the room, taking it all in.

"Wait," cried Zoo, "did you hear that?"

Brian nodded, "it sounded like a woman talking."

They looked wildly around the room, until a shelf crashed to the floor at the opposite end of the room, and they spun to look. Clouds of dust had flow into the air, and the cloud boiled as if someone was fanning the air.

Zoo got out his Kinect camera, and they saw a stick figure waving its hand, as if to clear the dust.

"We've got contact," he said, moving the device side to side to see what else was there.

And addressing the ghost, "Who are you? Why are you here?"

The dust cloud swirled, and the Kinect camera went blank.

He moved in back and forth in wider arcs each time, but the camera stayed blank.

Brian grunted and wrapped his arms around him, "I felt something brush by me."

Zoo headed toward the door they'd come in, and it started closing.

He caught the door before it shut fully, and felt it resisting his efforts to open it back up.

"Brian, give us a hand?"

He jogged over and together they managed to pry it back.

Zoo turned the corner, and heard something run up the stairs.

A mostly broken stained glass window shone blood-coloured fragments of light on the fuzzy strings of cobweb hanging from the banisters and moulding on the ceiling.

It was likely there was carpet underneath all the dust, but it was indistinguishable from the indeterminate pattern of the wallpaper.

"Did you hear that?" he looked at Brian.

"Sounded like someone walking up stairs."

Brian took his thermal camera from his tool belt and held it up to the landing, "cold spot on the landing.

"Moving upstairs."

Zoo paused to let them film the stairwell, then walked up the stairs, testing each tread fully before trusting it with his weight.

The rest of the team followed.

The door to the Master Suite was opposite the stairway, and when they got up the stairs, the door swung open invitingly.

The roof of the master suite had partly caved in, and grass was growing on the bed. The rest of the furniture around the walls was covered in dust, but appeared sound.

Zoo opened a drawer in the dressing table, "look, there's still clothes in the dresser." He paused for Steve to film it, then shut the drawer without touching them.

They looked at the top of the dresser, "some kind of green perfume bottle, compact, lipstick. Looks like they left in a hurry."

Despite the filth, the cheerful, sunny curtains, were perfectly still against the smashed windows.

"Try the Spirit Box?" asked Zoo.

Brian nodded, and pulled it out of his belt

Zoo asked again, "who are you? Why are you here?"

Static burst from the box, "Henry," followed by more static.

"Are you Henry Fox?" asked Zoo.

"Henry."

"What happened to you?"

"Where's Henry?"

Zoo frowned at the camera, "if this isn't Henry, then perhaps it's Morag Clementine, who'd been married just a few hours before she mysteriously disappeared.

"The police investigation at the time was inconclusive; no evidence of kidnapping, and no evidence of theft. The Detective in charge, an Inspector Morrison, noted his opinion that she'd absconded in the file."

"Talk to us Morag," begged Brian.

"Henry."

"Did Henry kill you?" he asked

"Henry.

"What happened to Henry?" Zoo demanded.

"Help.

"Scared."

Zoo and Brian looked at each other, then Zoo moved onto look at a picture of a young couple on a beach somewhere.

He couldn't help himself from straightening the picture, and his teamed smiled at each other.

Then it fell down.

They felt the atmosphere change and stiffened.

Zoo picked it up and tried to rehang it, but it slipped from his hands and fell a little further away.

He took a step forward, reached to pick it up, and fell through the floor face first to the sitting room below.

He lay stunned for moment, the dust half choking him, then asked, "Brian, are you there?"

There was no reply, and he struggled to turn over.

As the dust cleared, he saw a woman and a dog looking down through the hole at him.

"Careful," he said, "the floor isn't safe."

"No kidding," she replied.

"Wait, you're not real."

"Under ordinary circumstances I would be offended by that comment, but you're probably right."

"Who are you?

"Morag Clementine. I mean Fox."

Zoo cautiously sat up, "Am I dead or what?"

"Why are you asking me?"

"Aren't you a ghost?"

"I don't know, what's the date?"

"The date? What does that have to do with anything."

"Hold on a second, I'm coming down."

As he struggled to his feet, he heard her clattering down the stairs, followed by the dog.

She was wearing an old-fashioned dress, "you're the 1905 Morag Clementine?"

"1905?"

"Well, you can't be the 1905 disappearance and the 2030 as well."

"Why not?"

"Well, surely the original would be dead by the time the 2030 version was born."

"Ah, I see. You're assuming they're different people. Follow me."

She walked out of the drawing room, dog trotting behind and ducked behind the stairs.

He followed her out the door, and stood transfixed by the sunlight shining through the unbroken stained glass. He could fully appreciate the vibrant reds and greens of the twisted vine pattern.

The roof had a kind of moulded plaster leaf pattern which solved the Drawing Room ceiling mystery. The carpet was clean, with a discernible paisley pattern repeated on the walls.

Just moments ago, he'd seen it covered in generations worth of dust, and wondered what had been going on in Lucy Chalmers mind to let this go.

Morag popped out from behind the stairs, "Come along."

He followed her back to the servant's stairs down to the basement.

"What's with the dog?"

"I'm not sure how, but Dante found me."

"Found you?"

"Yes. What did you say the date was?"

"I didn't, December 17 2066."

She stopped abruptly, "December 17 2066."

He narrowly avoided walking into her.

She crossed a landing so small it was barely a corner and dropped down into the servants sitting room.

"What's so important about the date?"

"Hush, I'm thinking."

She waited until someone set a full cup of tea down, then picked it up and drained it.

"I can see why people thought the house was haunted. *Is* haunted."

She turned to look at him, "today's a total eclipse isn't it?"

"I don't know," he pulled out his phone to check, but the screen was blank, "out of battery."

"Probably not," she took a sip from someone else's cup.

"There was an eclipse the day I went back in time."

Zoo backed up and sat down. The person who'd been sitting on the chair sat up abruptly and backed away from it, "travelled in time?"

"Yes. Your two Morags are the same person.

"So there was an eclipse when I got here, an eclipse when I... phase shifted—"

"Phase shifted?"

"I don't know how else to explain it. I didn't die, and I didn't travel in time, I just kind of went invisible... Ah... Like a *Star Trek* cloaking device."

"*Star Trek?*"

"What? No *Star Trek* in your time?"

"No. I mean yes. It's just... Surreal."

Morag snorted, "aren't you supposed to be the great paranormal investigator?"

"How would you know that?"

Morag laughed, "are you dense? Your car is parked by the gate."

"Ah. Right. So eclipse for time travel and shifting."

"Right. Plus an eclipse when Dante found me," she stopped to scratch the dog's head, "and now an eclipse when you found me."

"So it's all about eclipses. How did you figure that out?"

"I did some research before I came back, only I didn't know I would get caught out. The weather conditions may have something to do with it. I can't research much further as I don't have the right kind of resources here."

"Can't you travel back to 2020?"

"I don't exactly know how I got here, but it seems I can't go back. At least, not until the conditions are right."

Zoo started to panic, "but where does that leave me?"

He looked into Morag's sympathetic gaze, "I don't know.

"But an eclipse lasts about five hours," she glanced at her watch, "if you're back in the same place, you might make it."

"*Might* make it? Shouldn't we get back up there?"

"If you like, I just wanted a cup of tea while I explained this."

He stood up and walked back to the stairs, turning to look at her as he reached the first step.

"Don't be such a wet week," she said "according to your reckoning I've been stuck here for 153 years and you don't see me complaining."

He turned back as she gulped someone else's tea, "how have you survived?"

She stood up, "I believe that *technically*, this is still my wedding day. So more to the point, what are you doing here gate crashing my big day?"

He preceded her up the stairs, "doesn't *The Ghost Detectors* car give it away?"

"Of course. We're a haunted house, she gave a lopsided smile, "it had somewhat of a reputation for that in 2020. That's why they had so much trouble getting a housekeeper. I suppose my disappearance made it impossible to get another."

She paused on the ground floor, "oh yeah, what about Henry?"

"He disappeared in 1922."

After a moment she started climbing again, "then, did he send me here to start this or to stop this?" she wondered.

"I'm sorry?"

"I met Henry in 2020, and he said everything started in 1904. He sent me back to stop it, but I've been thinking maybe he sent me back to start it."

"That's a bit stalkerish isn't it?"

"Well, it now seems my Henry came from 1922, and things were a bit different then.

"Though I have to admit I'd be creeped out if I hadn't just married him. Now that I have, it's more of a chicken and egg scenario. Did I send him forward, or did he send me back?"

Zoo tried to imagine where it started, "if you and the eclipse set up a time loop, when did it start?"

"And when does it end?"

"And how does it work?"

They went back into the Drawing Room. She looked up at the ceiling, then gestured at the floor, "about here I think."

He lay down, "there must be something more than the weather. The eclipse... say a low-pressure trough, and... lightning?"

As if on cue, a clap of thunder sounded overhead.

It went dark as the building shook more dust into the air.

"Yeah," Brian said from above him, "are you hurt, is anything broken?"

"Brian?"

The dust started settling, and Zoo could see Brian, Steve and Josh's heads looking through the hole in the floor above him.

"Careful," Zoo said again, "the floor isn't safe."

The heads disappeared, followed by footsteps on the stairs.

Steve got there first, "are you okay?" he asked, ever professional, still filming.

"Where's Morag?"

"Sorry?"

"Where's Morag?" he asked again as Brian and Josh arrived.

"There's no Morag, it's just us," said Brian. "Jeez mate, how hard did you hit your head?"

"But I met her, she said it was the eclipse."

He tried to get up, but Josh put a hand on his chest to hold him down, "Don't try to get up. I've called an ambulance."

Zoo struggled, "but Morag—"

"Don't try to talk either, you fell pretty heavily, you've probably got concussion."

"How long was I unconscious?"

"Don't be daft," said Brian, "you've only just fallen."

"But I met Morag, and she said it was the day she got married, and it was the eclipse."

"You couldn't possibly have done all that in the 30 seconds you might have been unconscious."

Zoo looked at Steve, camera still recording.

How desperate did he want to look on camera?

"Time dilation," he said, hoping that if Morag wasn't a figment of his imagination, she would hear. "Was it gravity, and not low pressure?"

He turned the camera off, and his crew did likewise.

The ambulance arrived, assessed the situation and secured a brace around his neck.

They asked the team to help with the stretcher, and about that time he blacked out for a moment.

As they wheeled the stretcher out, he looked up and saw a brightly lit Master suite window.

A woman leaned out and waved at him.

"Steve, the window," he said.

"What?" Steve craned his neck, "there's nothing there."

Zoo looked back as far as he could, to see what he could see.

Not her anymore, but definitely a lit window.

Did he have the ability to see paranormal phenomenon for real now?

As the ambulance crew wheeled the stretcher through the overgrown garden, he saw children laughing and playing, running through the trees.

Were they dead? Or had they been brought here by some unknown agency?

As he was loaded into the ambulance, he saw that it was full of people.

He did not need any one tell they were dead.

He screamed.

THE END

SPECIAL RELATIVITY IN SPACE

Space Mariner third class Kumahl Levi worked in a small cubicle.

It was a fairly standard ship cubicle, supplied with a small view screen capable of showing all of the cargo holds, and with his login, nothing else.

The communication system permitted ship-to-ship and ship-wide internal communications, but only private messages to the section heads.

Access to the ship's mainframe computer was only that required for the conduct of transport operations and nothing further.

The cubicle included a slightly broken black chair, and not enough elbow room.

Personal items were not permitted, so the grey cubicle was as blank, pristine and boring as the day it was made.

Only slightly more worn.

Thanks to his placement aboard the *AESV Albatross* he was working ship time; scheduled 6 hours on/12 hours off, instead of the 8/16 he'd be working in a placement back on Earth.

For the most part, his work was tedious and monotonous; he sat in his cubicle watching the transport panel.

And as he was the most junior transport officer, working through the "night" didn't help.

Thanks to the barely detectable hum and vibration of the engines, the slightly too warm temperature and the close, rebreathed ship atmosphere, his tiny workspace was soporific. Only the occasional flash of a light or ping of an alarm to keep him awake.

And of course, most of the interesting work, like pulling apart the transporter mechanisms, and performing routine maintenance happened during the swing shift.

With one hour of his watch left, there was one ship-to-ship transport scheduled.

Thankfully no training, and hopefully, no emergency drills during his off shift.

Now and again, he adjusted the wavelengths or time compensators and noted the calculations in the logs.

Or triggered automatic recalibrations.

Or a manual one for something a bit different.

All the major repairs and refits were done in the ship yard, so precious little of that to do.

There hadn't been a serious incident this tour, but he was so bored he almost wanted some kind of emergency situation.

Despite the monstrous amount paperwork that would require.

As if on cue, a burst of static heralded the transport.

"*AESV Albatross* this is *AESV Mermaid*, do you read?"

"Yes *Mermaid*, I read you."

"I have one standard container to transfer."

"I can receive one standard container. You have permission to enter the loading zone."

"Confirmed. Please prepare *Albatross* for loading."

"*Mermaid*, I can receive in five minutes on my mark," Kumahl set a stopwatch for five minutes and ten seconds, and at five seconds he started counting down.

"Five. Four. Three. Two."

"Mark," they said together.

"*Albatross*, I am sending the cargo manifest."

After a short pause, Kumahl confirmed, "I have received the manifest."

The transport appeared in the loading bay as expected, so he started the contamination scans.

"*Mermaid,* I have received your transport, and am initiating scans."

"I understand."

And that's where it started getting complicated.

The biohazard warning flashed and pinged, and for something to while away the last few minutes of his shift, he ran a detailed analysis to determine the hazard rather than just venting the atmosphere to destroy it.

And that's where it started getting puzzling.

Because the biohazard was human.

And if the analysis was correct, a human female.

A living human female.

Alone.

In deep space.

Well, not deep space exactly, but a vacuum sealed shipping container, that shouldn't in theory, contain humans.

According to interstellar law, all ships had a clear duty to help those in distress in space.

And there had been recent reports of human smuggling to the outer colonies.

And this was an Allied Earth Shipping Vessel...

He sent alarms to security and deckhands, an alert to the Captain and hailed the other ship.

"*AESV Mermaid*, this is *AESV Albatross*, do you read me."

"Yes *Albatross*, I read you."

"The shipping container includes a human female that is not in the cargo manifest."

"Say again please."

"Your shipping container includes a human female, not in the manifest."

"Kumahl are you pranking me?"

"No Seth. Unless there is an error in the scanning, a human is in the container."

"Confirmed. I will seek further information. Please stand by."

Internally, a security squad in protective suits arrived in the cargo hold and held a buzz of backward and forward comms with the dockworkers.

Kumahl knew it was there, but couldn't hear it.

He watched them preparing to break into the container.

As security stood, weapons at the ready, the dock workers brought in the heavy-duty laser cutters, cut through the lock, and opened the doors.

There was a pause; presumably security was demanding an orderly exit of the container.

A woman walked out with her hands up.

She wasn't wearing a ship suit, but weirdly in this day and age, an old-fashioned ankle length dress.

With what looked like lace on it.

An armed officer darted forward to secure her for the medical check and further interrogation.

"*Albatross*, I can confirm the woman was not detected in the departure scan. Are you sure there's one there?"

"I can confirm. I am looking at her."

"I will send you the scan."

After a couple of minutes, Kumahl confirmed, "I have received the scans."

He ran a quick eye over the scans, "I will seek further information. Please stand by."

He copied the information to the Captain, requesting departure clearance for the *Mermaid*.

It seemed an open and shut case.

The woman was not in the container when it left, and was somehow beamed in during the transfer.

It was an enormous risk; if the calculations were off by a fraction of a second, she'd be floating dead in the vacuum of space.

You had to admire that level of precision.

He watched as she was escorted from the cargo hold and the Captain returned permission to depart.

"*Mermaid* you are cleared to depart."

"I am underway. Let me know what happens with your mystery human."

"Will do. *Albatross* out."

And that was the end of the matter as far as Space Mariner third class Kumahl Levi was concerned.

He logged the activity of the day as far as transport was concerned, and closed out his station ready for the next shift transport officer.

Greater minds than him would look at how the woman had achieved the transport.

It was an interesting mystery, and he looked forward to reading the reports.

Assuming they weren't classified.

In the meantime, he was off shift, and after that level of excitement, he needed a beer.

Or two.

《《 • 》》

Morag Clementine understood the need for security.

After all, as far as they were concerned, she'd just materialised out of nowhere.

But did they have to be quite so rough?

And tie the restraints quite so tight?

And literally throw her in the brig?

At least that what she assumed this cold feature-less room was.

It was all smooth metallic grey, like brushed steel - floors, walls, ceiling. The joints between the walls and the floor and ceiling were featureless, concave surfaces.

It was disorienting, like being in a grey bubble.

There was no where to sit, or lie down, and noth-ing to do.

She'd always considered herself a law-abiding cit-izen, and for the most part, leaving aside a few pirated TV shows, smoked joints and occasional speeding, had always done the right thing.

That an armed squad who was so impolite as to be considered rude was in charge of her had come as quite a shock.

On top of what had already been a full day, she was exhausted.

She'd got married that morning, phase shifted in the afternoon, and now, teleported into a shipping container in the evening.

To say it had been a full day was an understate-ment.

She was about dead on her feet, and expecting her day to get worse, so she curled up on the floor and took a nap.

It seemed she'd just dozed off when she was woken by a hiss of gas in the room.

For an instant she imagined something like Zyklon B, but after a few moments of not choking, was reassured.

Perhaps it was reasonable of the guys in sealed suits to assume she was a carrier of something.

Not that she knew anything about the ship, but as an Australian citizen, was aware of the disastrous consequences of injudicious imports; cane toads, foxes and Indian myna birds to name a few.

Not to mention quarantine breaches like fire ants, European Wasps and Mediterranean Fruit Fly.

There was definitely a great deal to be said for biosecurity controls.

Or offshore detention for asylum seekers, but that was a different kind of security concern, one she didn't agree with.

The gas had barely stopped hissing before waves of coloured lasers bathed the room from top to bottom, and bottom to top.

She felt a tiny pinprick, like an insect bite, and rubbed her arm as the lasers ceased their display and the fog was sucked back out of the room.

After a while she gave up her expectation of immediate action, and went back to sleep.

《《 • 》》

Kumahl was woken early by a crewman with orders to attend the Captain's ready room.

Immediately.

Not that you ever really changed into pyjamas during a tour so that wasn't a problem.

But he had to prepare the bed for the next watch, splash water on his face and brush his teeth which took a little more time than immediately.

No time for coffee before scuttling down the passageways either.

All too soon he was knocking on a door, waiting for permission to enter.

"Enter."

Kumahl straightened his uniform hat, pulled his tunic down, and took a deep breath.

He opened the door, shut the door, took two paces forward and saluted the Captain.

She was standing at the map table with two women and a man.

Going by the uniform insignia, three officers, perhaps even her Command Executives.

"At ease," she said.

Kumahl relaxed, spread his legs a little and folded his hands together in front of his hips.

"Levi, I understand you have some knowledge of temporal effects on subatomic particles?"

He was puzzled by the question, "my Doctoral dissertation was on the astrophysical effects of long-term gravitational time dilation on subatomic particle cohesiveness Sir."

"And I understand Professor Smythe was impressed by your innovative treatment of gravitational time dilation?"

Curiouser and curiouser.

"Ah, yes Sir."

"And you co-wrote a paper that is still debated in academic circles?"

"Er, yes, but I'm not sure..."

The Captain glanced at each member of the group, and they nodded back.

"Let me introduce you to Chief Medical Officer Yang," she said, pointing him out on her left.

"Security Chief Singh," the woman in the centre.

"And Chief of Logistics McMasters," the woman on the right.

Kumahl stepped his feet back together, and saluted each in turn. They nodded back.

He relaxed again, curiosity eating him alive.

"We've been discussing the young woman from the shipping container," the Captain continued.

"Doctor Yang says she's in good health, and not a biothreat to the crew.

"Chief Singh has run a DNA scan, and she's not in any known database. Ordinarily we'd conclude she's a separatist, therefore suspect her motives in getting on board the *Albatross*.

"But Chief McMasters, has detected anomalies in her subatomic particles, and we're not sure what that means right now."

Kumahl nodded, but didn't say anything, though he had an idea where this was going.

"We'd like you to talk to the woman, who claims to be from 1905, see what you make of her story and come back to us on this."

"Yes Sir."

"Now, we don't want this getting out into the crew."

"No Sir."

"So until the situation is resolved, we're relieving you from transport duty, and explaining this as punishment for bringing an undocumented traveller on board."

"Yes Sir."

She smiled, "you will of course be working first shift for this project, and will report regularly to me.

"Yes Sir."

"Now," she checked her watch, "she should be about done with the quarantine protocols in pod one, why don't you escort her to Medical Observation Suite Four and organise breakfast for her?"

"Yes Sir."

"For the duration, we've allocated science lab two for you to work in."

It was the small, reputedly out-of-date lab.

The least visited, and the most out of the way lab.

And now he finally understood it was for secret projects

"Yes Sir," he saluted and left the room before they could change their minds.

But as he made his way down the passageways to quarantine pod one, he was jubilant enough to do a little dance.

Well, finally, something worth saying in his personal log.

And finally, his dissertation had some real-world repercussions.

It was kinda what he'd gone into space for.

But as he stood outside the pod, he became nervous.

What would this woman from the past be like? Did he need to be extra sensitive?

He knocked on the door, waited a moment, then opened it.

She had shoulder length red hair, and green eyes, and possibly freckles.

It was hard to say under the layer of dirt she and her dress were wearing.

She'd been trying to put her hair in order, and he'd caught her with her hands in her hair.

Trying to look nonchalant, she brushed some dust from the skirt of her dress.

"Hello," he said, "I'm Kumahl. I'm here to escort you to your temporary quarters."

She cocked her head at him, mimicking the sounds he'd made, and he realised she didn't understand Earth Standard.

He tried again in Earth English, "I'm Kumahl. I'm here to escort you to your temporary quarters."

Her face brightened, "I'm Morag. I don't suppose there's somewhere there to freshen up?"

"Freshen up?"

"Ah, this is going to be fun. Bathe"

As she saw his frown, she tried again, "Wash?"

"Shower?"

"Ah, I understand, there is a private cleaning cubicle in the room. Please come with me."

He left the room, and she followed, craning her neck up and down to see everything.

Pausing as they passed corridors, presumably noting the lack of other people.

"I don't want to seen ungrateful, but is there food in there as well?"

"There is not, but I will get you some."

They stopped at a door that looked very much like any other, and he opened it.

Inside, the room was spacious by ship standards, being roughly equivalent to a junior officer's room.

The single bed, dressed in white linens with a blue blanket rested on a set of drawers, one of them slightly open to reveal a ship suit.

At right angles to the bed, a drawer unit incorporated a fold down table, with a chair currently tucked under the table.

Next to that, a small upright locker, containing the sink, toilet facilities and shower.

The walls, furniture, ceiling, as well as the warren of pipes attached to the ceiling were painted cream to reflect the one light housed in the ceiling.

Morag looked dismayed, and Kumahl hasted to re-assure her, "this is spacious compared to mine."

"Really?"

"Yes, I have a berth I share with two others and one small locker."

"Actually, I was looking at the shower unit."

"Ah, well, it's small, but it's all yours. You won't be sharing it with a third of the crew complement. And it allows us to monitor your medical state."

"I see. And am I a prisoner here?"

"Not a prisoner, but not at liberty to leave until we've managed the risks associated with you being here.

"For you, as well as for us."

"I understand. Like when the Spanish brought smallpox to Mexico and decimated the Incan empire."

He puzzled through her language for a moment, and then said, "exactly. Or in this instance, more that we infect you."

"I'll leave you to bathe, and will return with break-fast."

《《 • 》》

Morag took a quick, and uncomfortable shower, and dressed in the ship suit.

It was like one of those pairs of active socks that are too tight when you first put them on, but adjust as your body warms the fibres up.

It was quite form-fitting, and having become accustomed to dressing in looser, less revealing clothes over the last year, she felt quite exposed.

She crossed her fingers and washed out her dress and underthings, hoping whatever the detergent was wouldn't ruin the dress because it had cost a fortune.

And it was her wedding dress.

And by the time she was done, Kumahl was knocking on the door. She raced to open it before he could let himself in.

Which was just as well, because he'd brought food. Something that looked like eggs, toasted bread, and some kind of salad. With a knife and fork.

And something that smelled like coffee, and tasted divine.

She didn't dare ask if any of it was fresh or recycled; she just pretended it was fresh.

Even though she knew it probably wasn't.

"Do you have a computer with whatever the Internet looks like right now?" she asked, sitting at the desk and tucking into the eggs.

"I'm pretty sure computers didn't come about until the late twentieth century."

She looked up absently as she munched. "No, I think my parents got their first computer in the late 1980s."

"But if you come from 1905 as you claim?"

"Ah, I see where you're going. It's a long story."

"I have plenty of time," he said, sitting on the bed and pulling a phone out his pocket.

Which was disappointing because she was expecting something a bit more Trekish.

Attempting to martial her thoughts, she picked up the coffee mug, and tucking her hand through the handle, cradled it in both hands.

"Right then." She took a sip of the coffee, "it was 2020 when I took a job at Hayward Hall in Melbourne. The Australian Melbourne.

"I met Henry Fox at the Hall. He and the Master Suite were trapped in some kind of time space loop on September 9th, 1904.

"Every day he woke up in a different time and place, but couldn't get back through the bedroom door."

He nodded as she got up, typing into his phone, thumbs flying. She picked up a piece of toast, and started pacing the room.

"I did some research, and I thought it was something to do with the lunar eclipse in conjunction with a low-pressure system and maybe a thunderstorm."

He nodded again, still tapping away.

On her way back she picked up the coffee again.

"On the 25th of November 2030, the atmospheric conditions were similar to those of September 9th, 1904 so we agreed I'd try to go back in time and stop him from starting that life."

He nodded, and she picked up the salad, ready for the tiny circuit of the room.

"I broke into the Master Suite, exactly as Henry described it, arriving in 1904, and a year later I thought I'd done the job.

"Then on August 30, 1905, the conditions were similar again.

"During a thunderstorm, I was in the Master Suite when I somehow phase shifted. I was there, but no one could see me."

She took a shuddery breath, rubbed her eyes that had started to water, and sat down again with a thud.

"Except Dante. Did you happen to find a dog anywhere?"

"I'm sorry."

"Poor Dante. He was a good dog. I'm going to miss him."

She wrestled for control of herself, and largely succeeded.

"Then I met a guy called Zoo, who said the date was December 17 2066. There was a thunder storm, and he said something about gravity before he disappeared.

"Or maybe I disappeared," she waved an arm around the room, "and arrived here."

Kumahl leaned forward, "so what was the date you left?"

"August 30, 1905"

"So, for you, time didn't move, but outside of you, time continued to pass. What about Henry?"

"Zoo said Henry disappeared in 1922, but I don't know anything about the circumstances."

Morag was suddenly exhausted, "I feel like this has been the longest day of my existence. I need a nap."

Kumahl jumped to his feet and waggled his phone at her. I've got enough to get started with some research, so I'll let you sleep, and come back later.

Which was a little funny, because that was almost the same as she'd told Henry, whenever that was.

《《 • 》》

As he made his way to the Lab, Kumahl was excited by the puzzle. Seemingly she'd been the victim of some kind of cosmic event, but how?

Was it the eclipse? What was it about the passage of the moon between the earth and the sun? Fluctuating atmospheric conditions?

Was it the weather? Particularly a massive injection of energy into the atmosphere via lightning.

Was there a gravity well? You need a lot of energy to escape a gravity well. You'd need to calculate the energy expenditure against the gravity based on where you were and where you wanted to go.

Then you'd need to choose the kind of propellant, in this case lightning, so you could calculate how much propellant you needed.

But lightning's an unreliable energy source, with variances in voltage and current. The power is also brief but large; a 10-microsecond burst of 5 gigajoules would result in 500 terrawatts of power.

You could store some of the strike energy in a capacitor, but you'd need to shunt off everything that was so high it might damage the capacitor.

Then again, the energy of a lightning strike is often dissipated into the atmosphere before it hits the ground.

Theoretically, you could draw lighting with a laser induced plasma channel, though you'd need a lot of energy to pull the lightning in.

So, there was a more or less obvious link between the lightning and a potential gravity well, but what was the significance of the total eclipse? Was it something to do with the moon's ascending node?

It seemed significant that it had all occurred in the same place, so his first step was to check the history of Hayward Hall.

Incredibly, the property was still there, only now it was a kind of psychic retreat and training centre with an on-site observatory.

The original core of the house was still there, surrounded by small accommodation units; scientists on one side, and psychics on the other.

He checked through the registry of owners, noting the transfer of ownership through the Foxes to the renowned astrophysicist Dr Paul Maidenwell, and on to the Maidenwell Trust.

In fact, Maidenwell had gone some way towards reclaiming the original grounds before he died, leaving a dedicated fund in his estate to continue the purchases.

What the hell had happened there?

It seemed Dr Paul Maidenwell had once been the host of a show called *The Ghost Detectors*, under the name Zoo, and during filming of the last episode he'd fallen through the ceiling and been injured quite severely.

After the show he'd bought the house and turned it into a business; initially as a haunted house theme park and later as the psychic retreat.

Before he died, he'd transferred the house into a trust with all his other assets and left it to be run as a going concern.

Now that he'd met Morag, he understood the stipulation the Master Suite remained unused; it was a sensible precaution to prevent anyone else being cast adrift in time and space.

Or perhaps, somehow preventing her return.

It seemed that after his encounter with Morag, he'd studied astrophysics under his real name; Dr Paul Maidenwell. He'd been one of the pioneers of research into special relativity.

And if Maidenwell had been focused on finding a way to bring her back...

Well, that was excellent; he could take it up where Maidenwell left off.

But out of curiosity, he calculated the earth standard date the container arrived, for Melbourne Australia. February 21, 2157.

He checked all the dates she'd given him:

- September 9, 1904, the date Morag arrived - total eclipse in the Saros cycle.
- August 30, 1905, the date Morag phase shifted - total solar eclipse in the Inex series.
- 1922, the date Henry disappeared - he'd wager that one would be September 21, another total eclipse in the Saros cycle.
- November 25, 2030, the date Morag went back to 1904 - total eclipse in the Saros cycle.
- December 17 2066, the date Dr Maidenwell met Morag - total eclipse in the Saros cycle.
- February 21, 2157, the date she's arrived in the container - total eclipse in the Saros cycle.

It was pretty coincidental that almost all the eclipses were Saros cycle but why was the phase shift an Inex cycle?

And why didn't any of the other Inex cycle dates trigger shifts?

Unless they did, but she was alone and didn't notice them?

The next date in the Saros cycle was February 21, 2175. The cycle started July 13 1219, lasting through to September 5, 2499.

Was it reasonable to assume she couldn't go further forward than 2499? That if she was before 1219 or after 2499, she would be safe?

Ack.

He needed to do something physical to make his brain move, so he booked an exercise pod with a treadmill.

But before he left the lab, he set off a computer programme to look for commonalities in the conditions on her dates.

And then to analyse all of the possible eclipses of any kind within the Saros date range, looking for additional dates with similarities.

As he ran, he considered the exercise pod; it was essentially an enclosure for a gravity field. Once closed, it could theoretically be relocated anywhere on the ship, but in practice, was suspended from the ceiling.

Could you rig one up as a kind of Faraday Cage to direct lightning away from a passenger, while using it as a method of propulsion? Like a kind of time capsule?

He abandoned the exercise pod, and jogged through the back passageways to the lab.

In a flow state, working through lunch, not noticing his hunger.

The computer had finished its analysis, returning a small set of variables that applied to each date.

In a few Earth days there was one date, out of sequence, with the right conditions.

So, the next thing to do was look at her physical conditions, starting with the subatomic scan.

Something about the phase shift had preserved her body's age in 1905. There were no signs of decay; she literally hadn't aged a day.

There was nothing to suggest she might experience rapid ageing on the other side, but it was a risk.

In fact, there was the potential that she would stay the same age forever.

Though it might be better to do a full set of medical diagnostics to see what they were working with.

He sent a brief report to the Captain on his findings so far, included a request for Morag to be given an internet accessible device, and the scans, as well as permission to begin fitting out a pod to send her home

Then he ate some lunch and organised a tray for Morag.

《《 • 》》

Morag was asleep, curled up on the bed like a cat.

"Morag," he called her name.

She didn't respond.

He called her name again, and touched her shoulder.

Still no response.

He shook her gently.

Still nothing.

He put a call into Chief Medical Officer Yang, who arrived moments later.

"What happened?" he asked.

"Nothing, that I know of.

"She took a shower, and ate a little breakfast this morning. She said she was tired, so I left her to sleep.

"That was about an hour after I left the Captain's Rooms this morning."

"All right," Yang pulled out his phone, "let's get rid of some of this furniture," he swiped his finger up and got rid of everything but the bed, which reverted back to a biobed.

He tapped a few times, and coloured lasers took the scans.

"This isn't looking good, there's been a deterioration in some of her core functions. I'll need to make some adjustments."

He tapped out a prescription in his phone, and swiped it towards the biobed, ejected a hypospray from the bed, and injected it into Morag's neck.

The scans continued; "it looks like some kind of time sickness. She's stabilising, but if she's going to survive, you'll need to send her back sooner rather than later."

Kumahl took a step back, "I've got an idea, but I can't do it for a couple of days, and I've no way of knowing whether it will work."

Yang put his hand on his hip, and gestured his phone at the bed. "She will die if she stays here. She might die when she goes back, but at least you'll know you did your best for her, so get to work."

《《 • 》》

Kumahl and Chief Medical Officer Yang laid the still comatose Morag, in the modified exercise pod and closed the lid.

The Captain, Security Chief Singh, and Chief of Logistics McMasters watched on.

They'd dressed her in the clothes she arrived with.

It felt cruel to let her go without saying something, or wishing her better, or giving her a small gift.

McMasters handed Kumahl the control mechanism, and as he activated the pod, the Captain said, "have a safe journey."

The pod disappeared with a sucking noise and a pop.

She was gone, and it was a moot point whether Kumahl would ever know what had happened to her.

He looked, but couldn't find any other references to her after her 2030 disappearance.

But Yang was right, he had done his best for her.

And earned a field promotion.

Morag landed with a thump.

The capsule fell open and she spilled out.

As lightening played over it, it fizzled and disintegrated.

She was found unconscious, deep in dense bushland, near Mount Donna Buang, East of Melbourne by bush walkers who called the Police.

The emergency services evacuated her by helicopter to the Royal Melbourne Hospital.

A small newspaper article mentioned the mystery woman who'd been discovered in bushland without her memory.

It was a sensational beat up with details of meteor showers and a supposed hovering UFO with allegations of alien abduction.

But Morag new better. She hadn't been abducted by aliens, but returned by Earthers from the future.

Not that she told anyone.

Ever.

THE END

ABOUT THE AUTHOR

Alexandria Blaelock writes stories, some of them for *Ellery Queen's Mystery Magazine* and *Pulphouse Fiction Magazine*.

She's also written four self-help books applying business techniques to personal matters like getting dressed, cleaning house, and feeding your friends.

As a recovering Project Manager, she's probably too fond of sticking to plan. She lives in a forest because she enjoys birdsong, the scent of gum leaves and the sun on her face. When not telecommuting to parallel universes from her Melbourne based imagination, she watches K-dramas, talks to animals, and drinks Campari. At the same time.

Discover more at www.alexandriablaelock.com.